'You are pregnant,' Ramon's voice turned a shade cooler. 'With *my* child.' He paced away, turned back. 'Would you relegate me to the role of a part-time father? Someone who breezes in and out of our child's life whenever the custody arrangement tells me I can?'

Emily felt her face blanch. That was exactly the kind of arrangement she'd assumed they would eventually agree upon. But Ramon's description made her blood run cold. Made her think of all the times she'd curled up on her bed as a little girl and cried, believing her daddy didn't care enough to visit her.

A fluttery, panicky feeling worked its way up her throat. 'But what about us?'

He clasped her shoulders. 'We're good together, *querida*. Are you denying that?'

'Lust is hardly a foundation for marriage.'

The hard line of his mouth softened. 'But it's a good starting point, *sí*?'

# Ruthless Billionaire Brothers

*These brothers have conquered everything—
except love!*

The de la Vega brothers may not be bonded by blood,
but these billionaires are united by their legendary
business success! Neither has failed in the acquisition
of wealth and power. But they're both about to realise
there might be one thing just beyond their reach…

Two irresistible women are about to interfere in their
well-laid plans—and the sparks that fly will result in
burning seduction!

Read Ramon and Emily's story in

*A Night, A Consequence, A Vow*

Available now!

And look out for Xavier and Jordan's story

Coming soon!

# A NIGHT,
# A CONSEQUENCE,
# A VOW

BY
## ANGELA BISSELL

First Published in Great Britain 2017
By Mills & Boon, an imprint of HarperCollins*Publishers*
1 London Bridge Street, London, SE1 9GF

© 2017 Angela Bissell

ISBN: 978-0-263-92490-9

Our policy is to use papers that are natural, renewable and recyclable
products and made from wood grown in sustainable forests. The logging
and manufacturing processes conform to the legal environmental
regulations of the country of origin.

Printed and bound in Spain
by CPI, Barcelona

**Angela Bissell** lives with her husband and one crazy Ragdoll cat in the vibrant harbourside city of Wellington, New Zealand. In her twenties, with a wad of savings and a few meagre possessions, she took off for Europe, backpacking through Egypt, Israel, Turkey and the Greek Islands before finding her way to London, where she settled and worked in a glamorous hotel for several years. Clearly the perfect grounding for her love of Mills & Boon Modern Romance! Visit her at angelabissell.com.

### Books by Angela Bissell

### Mills & Boon Modern Romance

*Irresistible Mediterranean Tycoons*

*Surrendering to the Vengeful Italian*
*Defying Her Billionaire Protector*

Visit the Author Profile page
at millsandboon.co.uk for more titles.

For Bron—author, mentor and friend.
Your support and encouragement have meant the world.

# CHAPTER ONE

'You owe me for this, Xav.'

Ramon de la Vega dropped into a chair in front of his brother's desk and stretched out his legs.

Eight hours on a transatlantic commercial flight, another hour in the back of a company limo inching through endless queues of bumper-to-bumper traffic, and he felt as if he'd been straitjacketed for a week.

His mood carefully harnessed, he lounged back and perched his feet on the corner of his brother's desk. 'I had planned to spend the weekend in Vegas,' he added.

His brother, Xavier, sat in a high-backed chair on the other side of the massive oak desk—an antique heirloom their father had handed down along with the company reins to his eldest son. Behind him a thick pane of wall-to-wall glass framed a sweeping view of Barcelona that drew no more than a brief, disinterested glance from Ramon. Instead, he focused on his brother, who looked impossibly cool and immaculate in a dark tailored suit in spite of the mid-August heat. As always, Xav's features were stern, his posture stiff. Only his right hand moved, his fingertips drumming an incessant beat on the desktop's fine leather inlay.

The sound, amplified by the dearth of any other in the vast corner office, penetrated Ramon's eardrums like a blunt needle and reminded him that flying and alcohol made for an unwise mix.

'Doing what?' Xav's voice carried the hint of a sneer. 'Gambling or womanising?'

Ramon ignored the disdain in his brother's voice and unleashed his grin—the one he knew could fell a woman at fifty paces. Or tease the tension out of an uptight client in a matter of seconds. Against his only sibling, however, the impact was negligible. 'It is called recreation, brother.' He kept his tone light. 'You should try it some time.'

The deep plunge of Xav's eyebrows suggested he'd sooner lose an arm than indulge in such hedonistic pursuits. His fingers stopped drumming—*mercifully*—and curled into a loose fist. 'Get your feet off my desk.' His gaze raked over Ramon's jeans and shirt before snapping back to his feet. 'And where the hell are your shoes?'

Ramon dropped his feet to the floor. His loafers were... He squinted, trying to remember where he'd left them. *Ah, yes.* In the outer office. Under the desk of the pretty brunette whose name had already escaped him. He considered the rest of his appearance: stonewashed designer jeans; a loose open-necked white shirt, creased from travel; and a jaw darkened by eighteen-plus hours' worth of stubble. A far cry from his brother's impeccable attire and his own usual standard, but a man had to travel in comfort. Especially when his brother had had the nerve to issue an urgent summons and then deny him use of the company jet.

Ramon made a mental note.

*Buy my own plane.*

At least the curvy redheaded flight attendant in First Class who'd served him meals and refreshments during the flight from New York hadn't minded his attire. But, yes, for the Vega Corporation's head office in the heart of Barcelona's thriving business district, he was most definitely under-dressed.

Still, Xav needed to chill. Cut him some slack. He had ditched everything, including a weekend in Las Vegas with his old Harvard pals, and flown nearly four thousand miles across the North Atlantic—all because his brother had called out of the blue and told him he needed him.

*Needed* him, no less.

Words Ramon had once imagined would never tumble from his proud brother's mouth.

Yet, incredibly, they had.

Beyond that surprising entreaty, Xav had offered no more by way of explanation and Ramon had not demanded one. As CEO, Xav technically outranked him but it wasn't his seniority that commanded Ramon's loyalty. Xav was family. And when it came to family there was one truth Ramon could never escape.

He owed them.

Still, he allowed his grin to linger. Not because his mood leaned towards humour—nothing about being back in Spain tickled his funny bone—but rather because he knew it would irritate his brother. 'Flying makes my feet swell,' he said, 'and your secretary offered to massage them while you were wrapping up your meeting.'

A look of revulsion slid over Xav's face. 'Please tell me you are joking.'

'*Sí*, brother.' Ramon broadened his grin. 'I am.'

Though he *had* got the impression as he'd kicked off his shoes and settled in for a friendly chat with… Lola?… Lorda?…that she'd happily massage a lot more than his feet if he gave her half a chance. And maybe he would if she was willing. Because God knew he'd need a distraction while he was here. Some way to escape the toxic memories that sooner or later would defy his conscious mind and claw their way to the surface.

Xav pinched the bridge of his nose, a *Lord give me patience* gesture that reminded Ramon of their father, Vittorio. Not that any likeness could be attributed to genetics: Xav had been adopted at birth by their parents after two failed pregnancies. Four years later Ramon had come along—the miracle child the doctors had told his mother she'd never conceive let alone carry to term.

Miracle Child.

The moniker made Ramon's gut burn. He hated it. He was no heaven-sent miracle. Just ask the Castano family, or the Mendosas. No doubt they would all vehemently agree and then, for good measure, throw in a few fitting alternatives.

Ramon could think of one or two himself.

Like Angel of Death.

Or maybe Devil Incarnate.

He snapped his thoughts out of the dark mire of his past. This was why he gave Spain a wide berth whenever possible. Too many ghosts lurked here. Too many reminders. 'Tell me why I'm here,' he demanded, his patience dwindling.

'There's a board meeting tomorrow.'

He frowned. 'I thought the next quarterly meeting was six weeks from now.' He made a point of knowing when the board meetings were scheduled for so he could arrange to be elsewhere. In his experience, day-long gatherings with a bunch of pedantic, censorious old men were a special brand of torture to be studiously avoided. 'Since when does our board meet on a Saturday?'

'Since I decided to call an emergency meeting less than twenty-four hours ago.'

Ramon felt his mood start to unravel. 'Why the hell didn't you say over the phone it was a board meeting you were dragging me over here for?'

'Because you would have found an excuse not to come,' Xav snapped. 'You would rather waste your time at a poker table—or buried between the legs of some entirely unsuitable woman!'

Ramon's brows jerked down. 'That's out of order,' he growled.

Abruptly Xav stood up, stalked to the window behind him and stared out. Ramon glowered at his back. Xav *was* out of order. Yes, Ramon avoided the boardroom. Pandering to the board, keeping the old cronies happy, was his brother's responsibility. Not his. But no one could deny that he gave his pound of flesh to the Vega Corporation. He'd done so every year for the last five years, in fact. Ever since he'd accepted the vice-presidential role his father had offered him on his twenty-fifth birthday. He'd side-lined his architectural career. Gone from designing luxury hotels and upscale entertainment complexes to buying them and overseeing their management.

He'd excelled—and he'd realised in that first year of working hard to prove himself that this was how he could repay his family. How he could compensate in a tangible way for the pain he'd inflicted, the destruction his eighteen-year-old self had wrought and the shame he'd brought on his family. He could stamp his mark on the business. Contribute to its success.

It had been a tall order. The de la Vega empire was well-established. Successful. It spanned continents and industries, from construction and real estate to hospitality and entertainment. Any contribution Ramon made had to be significant.

He had risen to the challenge.

First with his acquisition of the Chastain Group—a collection of luxury resorts and boutique hotels which had doubled Vega Corporation's market share on the European continent, and then with the expansion of their portfolio of private members' clubs into a lucrative network of sophisticated high-end establishments.

Yes, he had made his mark.

And yet to his brother—and most of the board—the spectacular results he'd achieved year upon year seemed to matter far less than how he chose to conduct his personal life.

It rankled.

He didn't deliberately court the press but neither did he

waste his time trying to dodge the attention. Evade one paparazzo and ten more would materialise from the shadows. It was easier to give them what they wanted. Flash his trademark grin at the cameras, drape his arm around the waist of a beautiful woman and the tabloids and their gossip-hungry readers would be satisfied.

But dare to deny them and they'd stalk you like prey. Look for scandal where none existed. Or, worse, where it *did* exist. And the last thing he needed was someone digging into his past and shining a spotlight on his teenage transgressions. Nurturing his playboy reputation served a purpose. The tabloids saw what he wanted them to see. A successful, wealthy, aristocratic bachelor who pursued pleasure as doggedly as he pursued his next acquisition.

He reined in his anger. 'Why an emergency meeting?'

Xav turned, his expression grim. 'Hector is making a play for the chairman's role.'

Ramon narrowed his eyes. 'I thought you and Papá had earmarked Sanchez for the role,' he said, referring to their newest and most dynamic board member—an accomplished former leader of industry who Xav had persuaded the board to accept in an attempt to inject some fresh blood into the company's governance. Aside from Xav and their father, who was about to retire as Chairman, Sanchez was the only board member for whom Ramon had any genuine respect.

Hector, on the other hand, was a nightmare. Their father's second cousin, he craved power and status and resented anyone who possessed more than he did. The man was self-centred. Narrow-minded. Not figurehead material.

Ramon shook his head in disbelief. 'He'll never get the support he needs.'

'He already has it.' Xav dropped into his chair, nostrils flaring. 'He's been working behind my back, garnering support for a coup. Persuading the others that voting in Sanchez is a bad move.'

'Surely Papá can pull him into line?'

His brother threw him a look.

'Papá has already taken a step back. He's too unwell for such drama—something you would know if you made an effort to visit more often,' Xav said, the glint in his eyes hard. Accusatory.

A sharp jolt went through Ramon. He knew their father had high blood pressure, and had suffered from mild attacks of angina over the past two years, but he hadn't been aware of Vittorio's more recent decline. He tightened his jaw against the surge of guilt. He kept his distance from family gatherings for a reason. There was too much awkwardness there. Too many things left unsaid. No. Ramon would not let his brother guilt trip him. He did everyone a favour, himself included, by staying away.

'The board members respect you,' he pointed out, marshalling his thoughts back to the business at hand. 'Win them back.'

Xav's jaw clenched. He shook his head. 'Whatever diamond-studded carrot Hector is dangling to coerce their support, it's working. Lopez, Ruben, Anders and Ramirez have all avoided my calls this week.'

Ramon dragged a thumb over his bristled chin. 'So what's the purpose of the meeting?'

'To confront Hector out in the open. Force him to reveal his hand and compel the others to choose a side—show where their loyalties lie so we know what we're up against.'

'"We"?'

'I need your support. As does Sanchez, if we've any chance of seeing him voted in as Chairman. We need to provide a united front. A *strong* front. One that'll challenge Hector and test his alliances.'

A single bark of laughter escaped Ramon. 'I cannot see

how my presence will help your cause,' he said, and yet even as he spoke he could feel the sharp, addictive surge of adrenalin he always experienced in the face of a challenge.

Something else rose in him, too. A sense of familial duty he couldn't deny. A compulsion to help his brother.

He studied Xav's face for a moment. It wasn't only anger carving deep grooves around his brother's mouth.

'You're worried,' he observed. 'Why?'

'The Klein deal went belly up.'

Without thinking, Ramon pursed his lips and let out a low whistle. Xav's expression darkened.

'I'm sorry,' Ramon said, his sympathy genuine. He too had suffered the occasional business failure. Had experienced the disappointment and utter frustration that came after investing countless hours of manpower and resources into a potential deal only to see it fall over at the eleventh hour. 'You're concerned that your credibility with the board is damaged,' he surmised.

'Hector's already laid the failure squarely on my doorstep. Called my judgement into question.' Xav's voice grated with disgust. 'He'll use it to undermine the board's confidence in me. We need a win to regain the board's trust. Something that will make them forget about the Klein debacle and give us some leverage.' He sat forward, his grey eyes intense. 'Have you managed to secure a meeting with Royce yet?'

Ramon felt his spine tighten.

*Speaking of failures.*

'Not yet,' he said carefully.

Xav leaned back, the intensity in his eyes dimming. He breathed out heavily. 'It was always going to be a long shot.'

His tone was dismissive enough to needle under Ramon's skin. Setting his sights on The Royce—one of London's oldest, most prestigious and highly exclusive private clubs—was ambitious, but his brother shouldn't be so quick to underestimate him.

'Have a little faith, brother,' he said. 'I've hit a minor roadblock, that's all. Nothing I can't handle.'

'A roadblock?'

'Royce has a gatekeeper.' He downplayed the matter with a one-shoulder shrug. 'Getting access to him is proving…a challenge.'

Xav's frown deepened. 'Do they not know who you are?' His voice rang with a note of hauteur. 'Surely the de la Vega name is sufficient to grant you an audience with Royce?'

Ramon nearly barked out another derisory laugh.

The importance of the family name had always carried more weight in Xav's eyes than his. Their mother and her siblings were distant cousins of the King of Spain and directly descended from a centuries-old line of dukes. Marry that blue-blood lineage to the vast wealth and success of their father's industrialist family and the de la Vega name, since the early eighties when their parents had wedded, had been inextricably linked with affluence and status.

'Are you forgetting the clientele The Royce serves?' He watched Xav silently bristle over the fact that their family's power and influence, while not insignificant, did not merit any special recognition in this instance. Not from an establishment that catered to some of the wealthiest, most powerful men in the world.

'And yet if there is truth to the rumours you've heard, Maxwell Royce is not selective about the company he keeps. Surely a meeting with you is not beneath him?'

Ramon sensed a subtle insult in that statement. He gritted his teeth for a second before speaking. 'It's not rumour. The information I received comes from a trusted source. It's reliable.'

As reliable as it had been surprising, for the discreet disclosure had come from his friend Christophe completely out of the blue. 'Royce has a gambling problem and mounting debts,' he said. 'It came from the mouth of his own accountant.' Who apparently, after indulging in one too many Manhattans in a London cocktail bar with a pretty long-legged accountant—who happened to be Christophe's sister—had spilled the dirt on his employer. Christophe's sister had relayed the tale to her brother and Christophe, never one to sit idly on useful information, had called Ramon.

'Where trouble resides, so does opportunity,' he said, voicing a belief that had served him well over the years when scouting out potential acquisitions. People resistant to selling could quickly change their tune when faced with a financial crisis. A buyout offer or business proposal that had previously been rejected could suddenly seem an attractive option.

The Royce had been owned by the same family for over a hundred years, but it wasn't uncommon for third or fourth generation owners to opt to sell the family business. For legacies to be sacrificed expediently in favour of hard cash. And if Maxwell Royce needed cash… It was an opportunity too tempting not to pursue, long shot or not. Ramon's clubs were exclusive, sophisticated and world-class but The Royce was in a whole different league—one that only a dozen or so clubs on the planet could lay claim to. An establishment so revered would elevate his portfolio to a whole new level.

Xav sat forward again. 'I don't need to tell you how much an acquisition of this nature would impress the board.'

Ramon understood. It would be the win his brother was so desperately seeking. A way to cut Hector's critical narrative off at the knees, wrestle back control of the board and regain the directors' confidence.

'Deal with Royce's gatekeeper, whoever he is, and get that meeting,' Xav urged. *'Soon.'*

Ramon didn't care for his brother's imperious tone, but

he bit his tongue. Xav was under pressure. He'd asked for Ramon's support. How often did that happen?

Not often.

Besides, Ramon had as much desire as Xav to see Hector at the company's helm.

He thought of the obstacle in his path.

Not a *he*, as Xav had assumed, but a *she*.

A slender, blonde, not unattractive *she* who had, in recent weeks, proved something of a conundrum for Ramon.

He'd readily admit it was a rare occasion he came across a woman he couldn't charm into giving him what he wanted.

This woman would not be charmed.

Three times in two weeks she'd rejected him by phone, informing him in her very chilly, very proper, British accent that Mr Royce was too busy to receive unsolicited visitors.

Ramon had been undeterred. Confident he could net a far more desirable result in person, he'd flown to London and turned up at the club's understated front door on a quiet, dignified street in the heart of fashionable Mayfair.

As expected, security had been discreet but efficient. As soon as he'd been identified as a visitor and not a member, a dark-suited man had ushered him around the outside of the stately brick building to a side entrance. Like the simple, black front door with its decorative brass knocker, the black and white marble vestibule in which he'd been left to wait was further evidence of The Royce's quiet, restrained brand of elegance.

Ramon had got quite familiar with that vestibule. He'd found himself with enough time on his hands to count the marble squares on the floor fifty times over, plus make a detailed study of the individual mouldings on the ornate Georgian ceiling.

Because she had made him wait. Not for ten minutes. Not for twenty, or even forty. But for an *hour*.

Only through sheer determination and the freedom to stand up, stretch his legs and pace back and forth across the polished floor now and again had he waited her out.

After a while it felt like a grim little game between them, a challenge to see who'd relent first—him or her.

Ramon won, but his victory was limited to the brief surge of satisfaction that came when she finally appeared.

'You do not have an appointment, Mr de la Vega.' Grey eyes, so pale they possessed an extraordinary luminescence, flashed at him from out of a heart-shaped face, while the rest of her expression appeared carefully schooled.

*Pretty*, he thought upon first impression, but not his type. Too reserved. Too buttoned-up and prim. He preferred his women relaxed. Uninhibited. 'Because you would not give me one,' he responded easily.

'And you think I will now, just because you're here in person?'

'I think Mr Royce would benefit from the opportunity to meet with me,' he said smoothly. 'An opportunity you seem intent on denying him.'

The smile she bestowed on him then was unlike the smiles he was accustomed to receiving from women. Those smiles ranged from shy to seductive, and everything in between, but always they telegraphed some level of awareness and heat and, in many cases, a brazen invitation. But the tilt of her lips was neither warm nor inviting. It suggested sufferance, along with a hint of condescension.

'Let me tell you what *I* think, Mr de la Vega,' she said, her voice somehow sweet and icy at the same time—like a frozen dessert that gave you a painful case of brain freeze when you bit into it. 'I think I know Mr Royce better than you do and am therefore infinitely more qualified to determine what he will—and won't—find of benefit. I also think you underestimate my intelligence. I know who you are and I know there's only one reason you could want to meet with Mr Royce. So let me make something clear to you right now and save you some time. The Royce is *not* for sale.'

Colour had bloomed on her pale cheekbones, the streaks of pink an arresting contrast to her glittering grey eyes.

*Interesting*, he thought. Perhaps there was a bit of fire beneath that cool facade. He held out his business card and took a step towards her but she reared back, alarm flaring in her eyes as if he had crossed some invisible, inviolable boundary. *Huh.* Even more interesting. 'Ten minutes of Mr Royce's time,' he said. 'That is all I am asking for.'

'You're wasting your time. Mr Royce is not here.'

'Then perhaps you would call me when he is. I'll be in London for another forty-eight hours.'

He continued to hold out his card and finally she took it, exercising great care to ensure her fingers didn't brush against his. Then she gave him that smile again and this time it had the strangest effect, igniting a spark of irritation, followed by a rush of heat in the pit of his stomach. He imagined kissing that haughty little smile right off her pretty face. Backing her up against one of the hard marble pillars, taking her head in his hands and devouring her mouth under his until her lips softened, opened and she granted him entry.

Carefully he neutralised his expression, shocked by the direction of his thoughts. He'd never taken a woman with force. He had no aversion to boisterous sex, and he'd indulged more than one bed partner who demanded it rough and fast, but on the whole Ramon liked his lovers soft. Compliant. Willing.

She took another step back from him, the flush of pink in her cheeks growing more hectic, her eyes widening slightly. As if somehow she'd read his thoughts. 'Mr Royce will not be available this week,' she said, her smile replaced now by a thin, narrow-eyed stare. 'So unless you have extraordinary lung capacity, Mr de la Vega, I suggest you don't hold your breath.'

And she turned and walked away from him, high heels clicking on the shiny chequered marble as she made for the door across the small foyer from which she'd emerged.

She had a spectacular backside. Somehow Ramon's brain had registered that fact, his gaze transfixed by the movement of firm, shapely muscle under her navy blue pencil skirt even as a wave of anger and frustration had crashed through him.

The sound of Xav's desk phone ringing jolted him back to the present. He shifted in his chair.

Xav placed his hand on the receiver and looked at him. 'Speak with Lucia on your way out,' he said. 'I told her to make a dinner reservation for us this evening. Get the details off her and I'll see you at the restaurant. We'll talk more then.'

Ah. Lucia. Yes, that was the name of his brother's secretary. Not Lola or Lorda. Ironic that he couldn't recall the name of the attractive brunette he'd just met, and had already considered sleeping with, yet he had no trouble summoning the name of the English woman he'd rather throttle than bed.

Her name, it seemed, was indelibly inked on his brain, along with the enticing image of her tight, rounded posterior.

*Emily.*

# CHAPTER TWO

EMILY ROYCE SAT behind her desk and took a deep breath that somehow failed to fill her lungs. For a moment she thought she might be sick and the feeling sent a rising tide of disbelief through her.

This was not how she reacted to bad news. Emily had learnt how to handle disappointment a long time ago. She did not buckle under its weight. When bad news came, she received it with equanimity. Practicality. Calm.

And yet there was no denying the sudden stab of nausea in her belly. Or the cold, prickling sensation sweeping over her skin.

She dug her fingers into the arms of her chair, some dark corner of her mind imagining her father's neck beneath her clenched hands.

*She was going to kill him.*

At the very least she was going to hunt him down, drag him out of whichever opulent hotel suite or illicit den of pleasure he was currently holed up in and yell at him until she was hoarse.

Except she wouldn't.

Emily knew she wouldn't.

Because no matter how many times in her life she'd imagined venting her anger, letting loose even a bit of the hurt and disappointment she'd stored up and kept tightly lidded over the years, she never had.

And this time would be no different. She would do what she always did. What she had to do. She would shove her emotions aside and pour all her energy into limiting the damage. Into doing whatever was necessary to sweep Maxwell Royce's latest indiscretion under the rug and in so doing keep his reputation—and, by association, the reputation of The Royce—intact.

Only this time, if what she had just been told was true, Maxwell had outdone himself. He'd created a situation so dire she struggled to accept that even he could have done such a stupid, irresponsible, *selfish* thing.

And this would not be a mere matter of slipping a wad of cash to some unscrupulous opportunist to prevent embarrassing, compromising photos of her father from finding their way to the tabloids. Or of dipping into her personal savings and hastily rebalancing the club's books, with the help of their accountant, to cover up Maxwell's misappropriation of funds from one of their business accounts.

Not that any of her father's prior indiscretions could be labelled trivial, but this…*this*…

Her grandfather would turn in his grave. As would his father, and his father before him.

Edward Royce, Emily's great-great-grandfather and a wealthy, respected pillar of British high society at the turn of the twentieth century, had founded the club on which he'd bestowed his name in 1904. Since then ownership of the prestigious establishment had been proudly passed down through three generations of Royces, all male heirs— until Emily. More than a hundred years later, The Royce remained a traditional gentlemen's club and one of western Europe's last great bastions of male exclusivity and chauvinism. A society of powerful, influential men who between them controlled a good portion of the world's major industries, not forgetting those who presided over governments and ruled their own countries and principalities.

On occasion Emily amused herself with thoughts of how the majority of their members would react to learning that fifty per cent of their precious club was now owned by a woman.

She imagined there'd be deep rumblings of discontent

and much sputtering of cigar smoke and Scotch beneath the lighted chandeliers in the Great Salon. But she also knew her grandfather had acted with calculated intent when he'd bequeathed half of the club's ownership to his only grand-child. Gordon Royce had known his errant son could not be trusted with sole proprietorship. Rewriting his will to leave fifty per cent of the shares to Emily—the granddaughter he'd wished had been born a boy—had surely been an un-desirable but necessary course of action in Gordon's mind.

Not that her grandfather had been able to overcome his misogynistic tendencies altogether. He'd gone to significant lengths to ensure the Royce name would live on through a male heir.

It was terribly ironic—that her grandfather should ma-nipulate her life from beyond the grave when he'd shown scarcely a flicker of interest in her while he'd been alive.

Emily closed her eyes a moment. Her mind was wan-dering. She needed to harness her thoughts, to wrestle her brain around the problem and come up with a solution. She needed time to think. Alone. Without the sinister presence of the man who sat in the upholstered chair on the other side of her desk.

She stood slowly, her features composed, her legs steady only through sheer force of will.

'I think you should leave now, Mr Skinner.'

She spoke with all the authority she could muster but her cool directive failed to have any visible impact on her visitor.

His head tilted to the side, his thin lips stretching into a humourless smile that sent an icy ripple down Emily's spine. 'That's a pity,' he said. 'I was just starting to enjoy our conversation.'

Emily didn't like the way he looked at her. Carl Skin-ner—one of London's most notorious loan sharks—looked old enough to be her father, yet there was nothing paternal in the way his gaze crawled over her body. She fisted her hands by her sides. Her pinstriped skirt and white silk blouse were smart and conservative and not the least bit revealing. There was nothing for him to feast his filthy eyes on, she assured herself—except maybe for the angry colour rising in her cheeks.

'Our conversation is over.' She gestured towards the single sheet of paper he'd produced with a smug flourish when she'd questioned the veracity of his claim. It lay upon her desk now, the signature scrawled at the foot of the agreement unmistakably her father's. 'I'll be seeking a legal opinion on this.'

'You can have a hundred lawyers look over it, sweetheart.'

Emily tried not to flinch at the endearment.

'It was legally binding when Royce signed it seven days ago,' he continued. 'And it'll be legally binding in another seven days when I collect on the debt.' He leaned back, his gaze roving around the interior of her small but beautifully appointed office, with its view overlooking one of Mayfair's most elegant streets, before landing back on her. 'You know, I've always fancied myself as a member of one of these clubs.'

Emily almost snorted. The idea of this man rubbing shoulders with princes and presidents was ludicrous, but she endeavoured to keep the thought from showing on her face. Skinner's business suit and neatly cropped hair might afford him a civilised veneer but she sensed the danger emanating from him. Insulting this man would be far from wise.

'Mr Royce's debt will be settled in full by the end of the week.' She injected her voice with a confidence she prayed wasn't misplaced. If her father's gambling debt wasn't settled within the week, the alternative—Carl Skinner getting his hands on a fifty per cent shareholding of The Royce—

was an outcome far too horrendous to contemplate. *She would not let it happen.*

'You sound very certain about that, little lady.'

'I am.'

Skinner's lips pursed. 'You understand that assurance would carry more weight if I heard it straight from your boss?'

'My boss is not here,' she reminded him, instinct urging her now—as it had twenty minutes earlier when he'd turned up without an appointment demanding to see her father—not to reveal her surname. She'd introduced herself simply as Emily, Administration Manager and Mr Royce's assistant, and agreed to meet with Skinner in Maxwell's absence only because instinct urged her to hear what he had to say.

She coerced her cheek muscles to move, pulling the corners of her mouth into a rigid smile. 'I'm afraid you'll have to settle for *my* assurance, Mr Skinner,' she said, walking around her desk as she continued to speak. 'Thank you for your visit. I believe we have nothing more to discuss at this point. I do have another appointment,' she lied, 'so if you don't mind…'

Skinner rose and stepped in front of her and Emily's voice died, her vocal cords paralysed by the violent lunge of her heart into her throat. Her legs froze. He was standing in her space, two feet at most between them, and she wasn't used to such close physical proximity with another person. Especially someone she didn't know and had zero desire to. 'Mr Skinner—'

'Carl,' he said, and took a step towards her.

She stepped backwards, glancing to the right of his thick-set frame to her closed office door. Her palms grew clammy. *Why hadn't she thought to leave it open?*

His smile returned, the narrow slant of his lips ten times more unsettling than before. 'There's no need to stand on ceremony, Emily. This time next week I could be your boss…'

Her eyes widened.

'And I'm not big on formality. I prefer my working relationships to be a little more…relaxed.'

Nausea bloomed anew and she fought the instinct to recoil. She tried to tell herself his sleazy innuendo didn't intimidate her, but the truth was she felt horribly unnerved. She inhabited a world dominated by men but she wasn't familiar with this kind of unsolicited attention. For the most part she was used to being invisible. Unseen.

She straightened her shoulders. 'Let me offer you one more assurance, Mr Skinner,' she said, her heart hammering even as common sense told her he couldn't pose any physical threat to her person. Her admin assistant, Marsha, unless she'd gone for her morning tea break, would be sitting at her desk right outside Emily's door, and Security was no further away than one push of a pre-programmed button on her desk phone. 'Not only will you never be my boss,' she said, a sliver of disdain working its way into her voice now, 'But you will never, so long as I have any say in the matter, set foot on these premises again.'

No sooner had the final word leapt off Emily's tongue than she knew she had made a grave mistake.

Skinner's expression had turned thunderous.

Terrifyingly thunderous.

And he moved so fast—looming over her, his big hands clamping onto her waist like concrete mitts as he pinned her against her desk—that she had no time to react.

An onslaught of fragmented impressions assailed her: the sight of Skinner's lips peeling back from his teeth; the dampness of his breath on her skin as he thrust his face too close to hers; the overpowering reek of his aftershave which made the lining of her nose sting.

Panic flared, driving the beginnings of a scream up her

throat, but she gripped the edge of her desk behind her and smothered the sound before it could emerge. 'Take your hands off me,' she hissed. 'Or I will shout for Security and an entire team of men will be here in less than ten seconds.'

For a moment his grip tightened, his fingers biting painfully into her sides. Then, abruptly, he released her and stepped away, his sudden retreat setting off a wave of relief so powerful her legs threatened to buckle. He ran a hand over his hair and adjusted the knot of his tie—as if smoothing his appearance would somehow make him appear less brutish.

'Seven days, little lady.' His voice was gruff. Menacing. 'And then I collect.' He jutted his chin in the direction of the paper on her desk. 'That's a copy, of course. You can assure your lawyer that I have the original tucked away safe and sound.' He sent her a hard, chilling smile then showed himself out, leaving her office door standing open in the wake of his exit.

Emily sagged against her desk, just as Marsha rushed in.

'My God!' the younger woman exclaimed. 'What on earth happened in here? The look on that man's face—' She stopped, her eyes growing rounder as they took in Emily's slumped posture and the pallor she knew without the aid of a mirror had stripped the colour from her cheeks. 'Emily…?'

Rousing herself, she pointed a trembling finger over Marsha's shoulder. 'Call Security. Tell them to make absolutely certain that man leaves the building.'

Marsha hurried back out and Emily moved on shaky legs to the other side of her desk. She picked up her phone, pulled in a fortifying breath and dialled her father's mobile number.

The call went straight to voice mail.

Surprise…*not*.

She slammed the phone back down, frustration, fury

and a host of other feelings she didn't want to acknowledge building with hot, bitter force inside her.

Her eyes prickled and the threat of tears was as unfamiliar and unwelcome as the nausea had been.

*What had Maxwell done?*

Her lips trembled and she pressed them together, closed her eyes and pushed the heels of her hands against her lids.

She knew what he had done.

He'd borrowed a monstrous sum of money to enter a high-stakes poker game and put up his fifty per cent shareholding of The Royce as collateral.

And then he had lost. Spectacularly.

She wanted to scream.

How could he? How *could* he?

No wonder he'd been incommunicado this last week. He was hiding, the coward. Leaving Emily to clean up the mess, like he always did.

Bitterness welled up inside her.

Why shouldn't he? She was his fixer, after all. The person who made things go away. Who kept his image, and by extension the image of The Royce, as pristine and stain-free as possible. Oh, yes. Her father might be a selfish, irresponsible man but he wasn't stupid.

He'd finally discovered a use for the daughter he'd ignored for most of her life.

Emily dropped into her chair.

It wasn't unusual for Maxwell to disappear. As a child she'd grown to accept his fleeting, infrequent appearances in her life, sensing from a young age that she made him uncomfortable even though she hadn't understood why. As an adult she'd hoped maturity and a shared interest in The Royce's future would give them common ground—a foundation upon which to forge a relationship—but within the first year after her grandfather's death it'd become clear her hopes were misguided. The loss of his father had not changed Maxwell one bit. If anything he'd become more remote. More unpredictable. More absent.

It was Emily who had run the club during his absences, assuming more and more of the management responsibilities in recent years. Oh, Maxwell would breeze in when the mood took him, but he rarely stayed at his desk for more than a few token minutes. Why stare at spreadsheets and have tedious discussions about staffing issues and running costs when he could be circulating in the restaurant or the Great Salon, pressing the flesh of their members and employing his innate silver-tongued charm?

Emily didn't care that her job title didn't reflect the true extent of her responsibilities. Didn't care that for seven years her part-ownership of the club had remained, by mutual agreement with her father, a well-guarded secret. She knew The Royce's membership wasn't ready for such a revelation. The club was steeped in tradition and history, mired in values that were steadfastly old-fashioned. Its members didn't object to female employees, but the idea of accepting women as equals within their hallowed halls remained anathema to most.

Emily had a vision for the club's future, one that was far more evolved and liberal, but changes had to be implemented gradually. Anything fundamental, such as opening their doors to women… Well, those kinds of changes would happen only when the time was right.

*Or they wouldn't happen at all.*

Not if Carl Skinner got his grubby hands on her father's share of The Royce. There'd be no controlling Skinner, no keeping the outcome under wraps. It would be an unmitigated scandal, ruinous to the club's image. There'd be a mass exodus of members to rival establishments. In short, there would be no club. Not one she'd want to be associated with, at any rate. Skinner would turn it into a cheap, distasteful imitation.

*Oh, Lord.*

This was exactly why her grandfather had bequeathed half of the club to Emily. To keep his son from destroying the family legacy.

And now it was happening.

Under her watch.

She reached for the phone again, imagining Gordon Royce's coffin rocking violently in the ground now.

Her first call, to the bank, told her what she already knew—they were at the limit of their debt facility. Raising cash via a bank loan wasn't an option. Her second call, to The Royce's corporate lawyer, left her feeling even worse.

'I'm sorry, Emily. The contract with Mr Skinner is valid,' Ray Carter told her after she'd emailed a scanned copy to him. 'You could contest it, but unless we can prove that Maxwell was of unsound mind when he executed the agreement there's no legally justifiable reason to nullify the contract.'

'Is there nothing we can do?'

'Pay Mr Skinner what he's owed,' he said bluntly.

'We don't have the money.'

'Then find an investor.'

Emily's heart stopped. 'Dilute the club's equity?'

'Or convince your father to sell his shares and retain your fifty per cent. One or the other. But whatever you do, do it fast.'

Emily hung up the phone and sat for a long moment, too shell-shocked to move. Too speechless to utter more than a weak, distracted word of thanks when Marsha came in, placed a cup of tea in front of her and said she'd be right outside the office if Emily needed to talk.

Alone again, she absentmindedly fingered the smooth surface of the pearl that hung from a silver chain around her neck.

An investor.

Slowly the idea turned over in her mind. There had to be members of The Royce who would be interested in owning a piece of their beloved club. She could put some feelers out, make a few discreet enquiries… But the delicacy required for such approaches and any ensuing negotiations would take time—and time was something she didn't have.

*Whatever you do, do it fast.*

Ray's warning pounded through her head.

Abruptly, she swivelled her chair, dragged open the middle drawer of her desk and rummaged through an assortment of notepads and stationery until her fingers touched on the item she was seeking. She held her breath for a moment, then shoved the drawer closed and slapped the business card on her desk.

She glared at the name emblazoned in big, black letters across the card's white background, as bold as the man himself.

Ramon de la Vega.

A bloom of inexplicable heat crept beneath the collar of her blouse. She'd intended to throw the card away as soon as she returned to her office after her brief encounter with the man, but at the last second she'd changed her mind and tossed the card into a drawer.

He had unsettled her.

She didn't like to admit it, but he had.

Oh, she knew his type well enough. He was a charmer, endowed with good looks and a smooth tongue just like her father, except she had to concede that 'good looks' was a rather feeble description of Ramon de la Vega's God-given assets.

The man was gorgeous. Tall and dark. Golden-skinned. And he oozed confidence and vitality, the kind that shimmered around some people like a magnetic force field and pulled others in.

She had almost been sucked in herself. Had felt the irresistible pull of his bold, male charisma the instant he'd stepped into her zone—that minimum three feet of space she liked to maintain between others and herself. She'd taken a hasty step backwards, not because he had repelled her, but rather because she had, in spite of her anger, found herself disconcertingly drawn to him. Drawn by the palpable energy he gave off and, more shockingly, by the hint of recklessness she had sensed was lurking beneath.

They were qualities that didn't attract her, she'd reminded herself sharply. Not in the slightest. And not in a man whose audacity had already set her fuming.

She leaned back in her chair, her breathing shallow, her pulse feeling a little erratic. Was she mad even to consider this?

Or would she be mad *not* to consider it?

Forced to choose between Carl Skinner and Ramon de la Vega, she couldn't deny which man was the lesser of two evils. De la Vega had a pedigree, not to mention an impressive business acumen. She knew because she'd done an Internet search and, once she'd got past the dozens of tabloid articles and photos of him with beautiful women, the long list of accolades lauding his accomplishments as both an architect and a smart, driven businessman had made for interesting reading.

Before she could change her mind, she snatched up her phone and dialled the mobile number on his card.

Two seconds later, she almost hung up.

Maybe this needed more thought. Maybe she should rehearse what she was going to say…

'*Sí?*'

The breath she'd unconsciously bottled in her lungs escaped on a little *whoosh* of surprise. For a second time that day, her vocal cords felt paralysed.

'Yes?' he said into the silence, his tone sharper. 'Who is this?'

Emily shook herself. 'Mr de la Vega?'

'Yes.'

'Good morning—I mean...' She paused as it occurred to her that he could be anywhere in the world—in a different time zone where it wasn't morning at all. She could have interrupted his evening meal. Or maybe it was the middle of the night wherever he was and he was in bed and... She froze, an unsettling thought flaring. Oh, no. Surely he wouldn't have answered the phone if...?

Before she could kill the thought, an X-rated image of entwined limbs and naked body parts—mostly naked *male* body parts—slammed into her mind.

She felt her cheeks flame. 'I'm sorry,' she said, mortified, even though he couldn't possibly know her thoughts. Where was her bulletproof composure? Skinner's visit must have unbalanced her more than she'd realised. 'I hope I'm not disturbing you. I'm—'

'Emily.'

Her breath locked in her throat for a moment.

'That's very impressive, Mr de la Vega.'

'Ramon. And you have a very memorable voice.'

Emily rolled her eyes. There was nothing special about her voice. There was nothing special about *her*. Ramon de la Vega was a silver-tongued fox, just like her father.

She sat straighter in her chair. 'Mr Royce would like to discuss a business proposition with you. Are you still interested in meeting with him?

'Of course.'

No hesitation. That was a good sign. She gripped the phone a little tighter. 'Nine o'clock tomorrow morning. Can you be here?'

'Yes.'

'Good.' She kept her voice professional. Courteous. 'We look forward to seeing you, Mr de la Vega.'

'Ramon,' he insisted. 'And I look forward to seeing you too, Emily.'

A flurry of goosebumps feathered over her skin. Had she imagined the sensual, lazy intonation to his voice that made her name sound almost…erotic? She cleared her throat. 'Actually,' she said, cooling her voice by several degrees. 'You may call me Ms Royce.'

Silence came down the line. In different circumstances, she might have allowed herself a smile.

Instead she hung up, before he could ruin her moment of satisfaction with a smooth comeback, and looked at her watch.

She had twenty-two hours to find her father.

# CHAPTER THREE

RAMON DIDN'T BELIEVE in divine intervention.

Only once in his life had he prayed for help—with all the desperation of a young man facing his first lesson in mortality—and the silence in the wake of his plea on that disastrous day had been utterly, horrifyingly deafening.

These days he relied on no one but himself, and yet yesterday... Yesterday he had found himself wondering if some unseen hand was not indeed stacking the chips in his favour.

And today—today he felt as if he'd hit the jackpot.

Because the thing he wanted, the thing he needed after Saturday's volatile board meeting, had just dropped into his lap.

*Almost.*

'Fifty-one per cent,' he said.

The indrawn breaths of three people—two men and one woman—were clearly audible across the boardroom table.

Ramon zeroed in on the woman.

Ms Emily Royce.

Now, that was a surprise he hadn't seen coming.

Though admittedly it wasn't a patch on this morning's bombshell: Emily was not only the daughter of Maxwell Royce, she was a fifty per cent owner of the club.

*Soon to be a forty-nine per cent owner*, Ramon amended silently.

'Absolutely not,' she said, the incendiary flash of her silver-grey eyes telling him she wasn't the least bit impressed by his proposal.

His London-based lawyer leaned forward in the chair

beside him. 'We appreciate you're in a difficult situation, Ms Royce—'

'I don't think you *appreciate* our situation at all,' she cut in. 'I think Mr de la Vega wants to take advantage of it.'

'Emily.' Ray Carter, the grey-haired lawyer sitting on her left, touched her briefly on the arm. 'Let's hear what they have to say.'

Ramon watched her right hand curl into a delicate fist on the table-top. Knowing what he did now, he wouldn't have been surprised if she felt inclined to punch the man seated on her right, nor could he have blamed her. No one privy to the conversation that had just taken place could deny that Emily Royce had a right to be furious with her father.

Ramon and his lawyer had listened, incredulous, as Carter had laid out the facts, stating his clients were making full disclosure of the circumstances in the interests of trust and transparency.

And then Maxwell Royce had offered to sell his fifty per cent shareholding in The Royce in exchange for a swift and fair settlement.

It had taken less than an hour for both parties to agree on what constituted 'fair'. Royce's need for an expedient, unconventional deal had given Ramon leverage that he and his lawyer hadn't hesitated to use.

But it wasn't enough. Ramon wanted a majority shareholding. Wanted the control that additional one per cent would afford him.

Ms Royce mightn't like it, but if she and her father wanted a quick bailout she *was* going to sell him one per cent of her shares.

And if she didn't quit glaring at him as if he were the Antichrist, instead of the man about to save her from a far less desirable outcome, he was going to crush any sympathy he felt for her and damn well enjoy watching her yield.

He looked into those luminous, pale grey eyes.

'I am not unsympathetic to your situation,' he said, ensuring his gaze didn't encompass her father. For Maxwell Royce he felt not an iota of sympathy. The man had been reckless, irresponsible. Ramon was a risk-taker himself, and no saint, but he'd learned a long time ago the only kind of risk worth taking was a calculated one. You did not gamble with something—or some*one*—you weren't prepared to lose. 'But I think we can agree that your options are limited and what you need is a fast and effective solution to your problem.'

He leant his elbows on the table, his shoulders relaxed under the charcoal-grey suit jacket he'd donned over the matching waistcoat, white shirt and maroon tie that morning. He spread his hands, palms up in a gesture of conciliation. 'I believe that is what I am offering.'

'Demanding a majority shareholding is not a solution,' she said. 'It's a takeover.'

Angry colour rose in her face, the pink contrasting with her pale eyes and accentuating the elegant slant of her cheekbones. With her blonde hair scraped into a tight twist behind her head she looked as prim and buttoned up as she had the first time he'd met her. But now he found himself conceding that Emily Royce wasn't pretty…she was beautiful—despite the *back off* vibe she radiated with her prickly demeanour.

He dropped his gaze to her mouth. Remembered the swift, unexpected urge she'd aroused during their first encounter—the powerful desire to kiss her, to soften that condescending smile into something warmer, more inviting.

No smile adorned her mouth this morning but the tight moue of her lips did not diminish his appreciation of the fact they were lush and shapely.

Rather like her body, the generous curves of which he couldn't fail to notice. Not when the soft, pale blue top she wore moulded her ample breasts and slender midriff to utter perfection. He wasn't blind. He was a thirty-year-old red-blooded man who liked the opposite sex. A lot. When a desirable woman drifted into his orbit, his body was programmed to notice.

He clenched his jaw.

Lust had no place in this meeting. He was on the cusp of achieving what his brother had believed he couldn't. He wasn't about to lose focus.

He'd satisfy his libido later. Celebrate with a night out in London and find himself a woman who was warm and willing, not stiff and spiky, like the one sitting opposite.

'Correct me if I am wrong, Ms Royce,' he said. 'But my understanding from Mr Carter's summary of the situation is that you and Mr Royce have less than six days to raise the money required to settle his debt.'

Emily glanced at her father. Royce looked impeccable in a pinstriped navy suit but his clean-shaven face was noticeably drawn, his blue eyes underscored by dark shadows. In the moment his daughter looked at him, something that could have been regret, or shame, passed over his features.

Her gaze came back to Ramon. 'That is correct.'

'Then I will present you with two options. You can refuse my offer and watch me walk out of here—' he paused for a beat to let that threat sink in '—or you can sell one per cent of your shares to me in addition to your father's fifty and I will execute the deal and wire the money within the next forty-eight hours.'

Her eyes narrowed. 'Just like that?'

'We have established there is no time for prolonged negotiations, have we not?'

'What about due diligence?'

He waved a hand. 'Give us access to your books today and we'll satisfy ourselves there are no major issues for concern.'

She eyed him across the wide mahogany table, her head tilting to one side. 'I'm curious about your interest in The Royce, Mr de la Vega. Your own clubs seem to be doing rather well but they're hardly in the same league. This establishment is built on a foundation of prestige and tradition and we cater to an elite and very discerning clientele. We are not a playpen for the *nouveau riche*.'

She was baiting him and Ramon counselled himself not to bite. His clubs were not *doing rather well*, they were reaping the rewards of extraordinary success. Yes, they were luxurious—decadent, even—but every aspect of their design embodied taste and sophistication. And they were wildly popular. His newest club, launched in Paris just four weeks ago, had reached its full membership quota six months before opening night and now had a waiting list of hundreds.

'The Royce is an icon in the industry,' he said. 'I assure you I have no intention of doing anything that would undermine its reputation.'

Her mouth opened but her lawyer sat forward and spoke first.

'Naturally Ms Royce is passionate about the club and preserving both its reputation and heritage. As a traditional gentlemen's club, it embraces values that are very conservative and, since female members are still prohibited, Ms Royce's part-ownership is not common knowledge.' He put down his pen and folded his hands on top of his legal pad. 'That said, she is an integral part of the business. If she were to agree to become a minority shareholder, we would seek a guarantee that her job remains secure. In addition, she would expect a reasonable level of autonomy in managing the day-to-day operations.'

Ramon inclined his head. 'Of course.' He turned his gaze on her. 'I have no wish, nor reason, to oust you from your business.' He wrote a number on his lawyer's note-pad, locked his gaze onto those pale grey eyes again and slid the pad across the table.

She leaned forward to look, as did Carter. The two exchanged a glance, then she picked up her pen, slashed a line through the number Ramon had written and wrote down another. She pushed the pad back to him.

He glanced down at the number.

'Done,' he said, and ignored the small, wheezy cough that came from his lawyer.

Emily stared at him, wordless.

'I suggest we make an immediate start on reviewing the financials,' he said smoothly. 'That is, if we're all agreed…?'

A hush fell as all eyes looked to Emily. Ramon waited. Her features were composed but he knew she waged an internal battle.

Finally, she looked at Carter, gave the briefest of nods then stood and walked around the table. She extended her hand. 'Congratulations, Mr de la Vega.'

He rose, wrapped his much larger hand around hers and registered at once the warmth of her skin. Surprise flickered. For some reason he'd imagined her touch would feel cold. Clinical. But the heat filling his palm was intense, almost electric.

Her eyes widened as though she too had felt something unexpected. Abruptly, she pulled her hand out of his. 'If you'll excuse me, I'll talk to our accountant and arrange for our financial records to be made available to you.'

'Thank you.'

She started to turn away.

'Emily,' he said.

She paused. 'Yes?'

He flashed his trademark smile. 'You can call me Ramon.'

* * *

Emily locked the door of the powder room, turned on the cold tap over the basin and shoved her wrists under the water.

She felt flustered, unbearably hot, and she couldn't understand why. Couldn't understand why Ramon de la Vega should have this crazy, unbalancing effect on her. Just being in the same room as him somehow had elevated her body temperature. Made her lungs work twice as hard to get enough air into them. And when she'd touched his hand... Her nerve endings had reacted as if she'd grabbed an electrified wire.

She dried her hands and sank onto a stool.

Had she done the right thing?

She closed her eyes and rubbed her forehead.

What choice had she had?

Ramon de la Vega or Carl Skinner.

In the end she'd had no choice at all. Her hand had been forced. First by her father's irresponsible actions and then by Ramon de la Vega's ruthless, self-serving agenda.

In less than two days from now, the Vega Corporation would own fifty-one per cent of The Royce.

*I'm so sorry, Grandfather.*

She exhaled a shaky breath.

At least Maxwell had finally turned up, although she couldn't have said whether it was an attack of conscience or the four messages she'd left on his phone, ranging in tone from pleading, to furious, to coldly threatening, that had prompted his appearance.

He'd looked terrible, as if he hadn't slept in days, and part of her had hoped he hadn't.

Why should he get the luxury of sleep when she'd lain awake all night worrying?

And then he had agreed to sell his shares.

It had taken Emily a full minute to realise the tightness in her chest had been not only shock, but sadness.

The Royce was the one remaining connection she had to her father. Now that connection would be irreparably severed.

She stood up suddenly and smoothed her hands down the sides of her trousers. She wasn't going to do this. She wasn't going to get emotional. It would only make her feel worse.

Drawing a deep breath, she headed down the plush carpeted corridor and looked into the accounting office.

It was empty.

Further along, she stopped at Marsha's desk. 'Do you know where Jeremy is?'

'He called in sick this morning.'

She sighed. The news wasn't welcome, and not only because she needed financial data from Jeremy. He was one of the few people at The Royce she felt able to confide in—and the only other person aside from Ray Carter who knew about her father's gambling problem. It would have been nice to talk with him.

Marsha looked at her. 'Can I help with something?'

'Do you have access to the finance drive?'

Marsha nodded and Emily grabbed a pen and a piece of notepaper and scribbled out a list. 'Download these files onto a flash drive and take them to our guests in the boardroom.'

'Mr de la Vega?'

There was a gleam in Marsha's eyes that Emily tried not to notice. 'Yes. And please also arrange for refreshments and lunch for our visitors.' She moved towards her office. 'Thanks, Marsha. I'm going to keep my door closed for a while. If Mr de la Vega or his lawyer ask for anything more, let me know.'

*So I can tell them to go jump.*

Except she wouldn't, because she didn't have that luxury. But the thought was satisfying, if nothing else.

Sitting at her desk, she forced herself to focus. This morning's outcome was not what she'd anticipated but she still owned forty-nine per cent of The Royce. She still had a job to do. The staffing budgets had to be completed and she'd promised the executive chef she'd look at his proposed changes to the seasonal menu and give her stamp of approval.

Plus there was the small matter of drafting a discreet communication to the members. Maxwell had agreed to a carefully worded announcement in his name welcoming the Vega Corporation as a shareholder. The members already believed he was the sole owner. Armed with only selective facts, they'd assume her father had retained the balance of the shares, and he and Emily and the club's new shareholder would allow that assumption to gó unchallenged.

It wasn't ideal, but discretion was necessary. The club's stability had to be her priority.

An hour later, despite her good intentions, Emily had abandoned her desk. She stood at her office window, her arms wrapped around her middle, her mind a tangle of thoughts as she stared sightlessly through the glass.

A knock at her office door jarred her out of her head. 'Come in,' she called over her shoulder, assuming it was Marsha.

It wasn't. It was her father.

She turned around and he closed the door, pushed his hands into his trouser pockets.

After an awkward silence, he said, 'The lawyers are fleshing out the terms. Ray will bring you a draft to review as soon as it's ready.'

'Fine,' she said, but it wasn't.

None of this was fine.

She wasn't fine.

Maxwell looked away first. He always did. 'If you don't need me—' he spoke to a point somewhere beyond her left shoulder '—I'll head off and come back when the agreement is ready for signing.'

*If you don't need me.*

Emily almost let out a bitter laugh.

Of course she didn't need him. She had needed him as a child, but he'd never been there, so she had taught herself to need no one.

'What will you do?' she asked, forcing the words past the sudden, silly lump in her throat.

He shrugged. 'I don't know,' he confessed, and Emily didn't think she'd ever seen Maxwell look quite so defeated.

'You still have the Knightsbridge apartment?'

Or had he gambled that away too? As he had everything else, including his father's stately mansion where Emily had lived at weekends and holidays when she wasn't at boarding school.

He nodded and, though she shouldn't care, she felt relieved that her father wouldn't be homeless.

He turned to go and all of a sudden Emily felt as if she were six years old and her daddy was abandoning her again. Walking out of the front door of the mansion and leaving her in that big, silent house with only her grandfather, his stern-faced housekeeper and her mother's ghost for company.

'Was it really so hard to love me?'

The words blurted from her mouth before the left side of her brain could censor them.

Maxwell paused, half turned. 'Excuse me?'

'Did you love *her*?'

She clasped the pearl at her throat and saw the tension grip her father's body. He had never talked about the woman who'd died giving birth to his only child.

'Your mother...' he began, and Emily's breath caught, her heart lurching against her ribs as she waited for him to go on.

But he simply shook his head.

'I'm sorry,' he muttered.

And then he left, closing the office door behind him.

*Gone.*

Just like all the times before.

Tightness gripped her throat and she blinked rapidly. *No tears*, she told herself fiercely. She returned to her desk, opened a spreadsheet on her computer and forced herself to concentrate. She hadn't allowed herself to cry in a very long time. She wouldn't start now.

Ramon draped his suit jacket over the back of the Chesterfield sofa in Maxwell Royce's soon-to-be ex-office and sat down. His briefcase, a sheaf of papers and his open laptop lay on the dark wood coffee table in front of him. He could have worked at the big hand-carved desk at the far end of the enormous office, but staking his claim before the deal was officially done felt a touch too arrogant, even for him.

He looked at his platinum wristwatch.

The lawyers had been hashing out terms in the boardroom for nearly two hours.

Trusting his own lawyer to nail down the finer details, he'd left them to it over an hour ago.

Several times since then he'd thought about seeking out Emily, but each time he'd curbed the impulse. This morning's meeting had been civil but tense. Allowing her a cooling-off period seemed sensible.

His phone buzzed and he pulled it from his pocket and checked the screen. Xav had sent a text:

Good work. Talk later.

He dropped the phone onto the table, annoyance flaring. After having sent his brother an update an hour and a half ago, he'd expected a more enthusiastic response.

He should have remembered Xav was not a man ruled by emotion.

The door to the office banged open. Jarred from his thoughts, Ramon looked up to see who had so abruptly intruded.

Emily.

Her fine features pinched into a scowl, she stood in the doorway with a sheet of paper clutched in one hand. She breathed hard, as though she had sprinted the length of the carpeted hall from the boardroom to the office. Her gaze found him and he felt the heat of her anger wash over him. Felt it reach into places he probably shouldn't have.

'Who said you could use this office?'

He rose to his feet. 'Your father,' he said, sliding his hands into his trouser pockets. 'Is that a problem?'

Stalking into the room, she raised the paper clenched in her fist. '*This* is a problem.'

He remained calm. 'Is my guessing what's on that paper part of the game?'

'This isn't a game, Mr de la Vega.' She threw the sheet of paper onto the coffee table and pointed a manicured finger at it. 'Care to explain?'

He glanced down. It was a page from the latest marked-up version of the agreement. He didn't need a closer look to guess which amendment had raised her ire.

He walked to the door and closed it. At her questioning frown, he said, 'We don't want the children overhearing our first argument, do we?'

Her eyes flashed, and the glimpse of a temper intrigued him. She grabbed the piece of paper off the table.

'We're not going to argue,' she said. 'You're going to take this to your lawyer—' she slapped the page against his chest, anchoring it there under her flattened hand '—and you're going to tell him to reinstate the bylaws under the list of matters that require shareholder unanimity.'

Ramon looked down at the slender hand splayed across his chest then back at Emily's upturned face. This close he could see the velvety texture of her long brown eyelashes and the rings of darker grey around the circumference of her irises.

When he breathed in, he caught a subtle fragrance that was musky and feminine.

For seconds neither of them moved.

Then, with her luminous eyes widening, she snatched her hand away, took a hasty step backwards and lost her balance.

Before she could fall, Ramon's reflexes kicked in and he caught her by the waist, hauling her against him. The paper fluttered to the floor and it took all of three seconds for his body to register the feel of her soft breasts against his chest, the shape of her delicate hips fitting to his.

His gaze went to her mouth. Her lips were no longer pursed in anger but slightly parted. A hot spark of appreciation ignited. When not taut with disapproval, those lips were sultry. Kissable…

'Stop.'

Emily's low, urgent command sent a jolt through Ramon. He realised he'd lowered his head—was millimetres away from satisfying his desire to know if she tasted as ripe and sweet as he imagined. He raised his head, noted the streaks of crimson over her cheekbones, the laboured quality of her breathing, and knew a rush of satisfaction.

The attraction was mutual.

She stiffened, even as she trembled. 'Let me go.'

His aroused body protested but his mind urged him to comply. He wasn't averse to mixing business with pleasure on occasion, but indulging his lust with the prickly

Ms Royce would be more complicated than a few hours or days of pleasure were worth.

Restored to his senses, he dropped his hands from her waist and stepped back.

She retrieved the paper from the floor and moved away, placing a good six feet of space between them. 'Is that how you settle disputes with your business partners?' Her face was flushed, her tone scathing. 'By kissing them?'

'Only the pretty ones,' he drawled.

She gave him a withering look. 'You're not funny, Mr de la Vega.'

'I thought I told you to call me Ramon.'

She flapped the paper in the air. 'And I thought you were serious about this deal.'

Her comeback sobered him. 'I am.'

'Then explain why you're proposing to curtail my voting rights.'

He pushed his hands back into his pockets. 'You want autonomy in the day-to-day operations,' he said. 'And I'm willing to grant you that. By the same token, as the majority shareholder I don't expect to need your agreement on minor policy changes.'

She sent him an incredulous look. 'Minor? The bylaws are hardly *minor*. They're the very foundation of the club. The rules and regulations that govern everything that's important to the members. Etiquette, dress code, membership—' She halted and, slowly, realisation dawned on her face. 'That's it, isn't it?' Her tone turned accusing. 'You want to push through a reciprocal membership arrangement with your own clubs.'

'No. But I do want to amend the membership protocols.'

Her eyes narrowed. 'Why?'

Because his brother needed leverage. Because it was an opportunity to counter Hector's underhanded power plays. Hector thought he could buy the loyalty of his fellow cronies, but what he failed to realise was that his supporters were no less duplicitous than he was. Offered the right incentive, they'd desert him in a heartbeat and give their allegiance to Xav.

And what better incentive than entry into a club where they'd rub shoulders with some of the most powerful, influential men in the world?

But first Ramon had to ensure there were no obstacles in the road.

'The approval process is archaic.' He went to the coffee table and picked up a bound copy of the club's rules and regulations. 'This says the protocol for accepting new members hasn't changed in more than sixty years.' He raised an eyebrow. 'Surely a review is overdue?'

She shook her head. 'You can't go changing the rules willy-nilly. The membership needs to be consulted. And the member who chairs the Admissions Committee is a stickler for tradition.' Her expression turned faintly smug. 'He won't be easily swayed.'

'Lord Hanover, you mean?' He smiled as the smugness slid from her face. 'A pleasant chap. At least, he seemed so when we spoke.'

Her mouth went slack. 'You…you spoke with Lord Hanover?'

'Briefly. Forty minutes ago. I've arranged to have lunch with him on Thursday.'

'You're *lunching* with Lord Hanover?' Her eyes narrowed. 'I don't believe you.'

He dropped the document, picked up his phone and started thumbing through his contacts. 'Would you like to ask his secretary?'

Emily snapped her mouth shut. 'Fine. I believe you. But aren't you jumping the gun? Our agreement isn't executed yet.'

He stilled. 'Are you suggesting it won't be?'

'Not in its present form.'

Tension clamped the back of Ramon's neck. 'There was a reason you called me yesterday,' he warned softly. 'Don't forget that.'

Her chin took on a mulish tilt. 'Are you saying this is a deal breaker?'

'Yes.'

Her head jerked back a little. Then she sucked in a sharp breath, crossed to the window and presented him with a perfect view of her long legs, graceful back and slender neck. Her blonde hair was still confined in a tight twist, but a few silky strands had escaped, and he was surprised to see how curly they were. He let his gaze slide lower. She wore black trousers that accentuated the gentle flare of her hips and, yes, her backside was spectacular.

She spun to face him. 'If I waive the unanimity requirement, I want something in return.'

He shifted his weight. 'Go on.'

'Grant my father an honorary position as chairman.'

He stared at her, his appreciation of her curves swiftly forgotten.

'Plus a modest monthly allowance.'

His disbelief ballooned. Sharp on its heels came a surge of anger. 'Your father's actions have jeopardised the future of this club, and you want to reward him with an honorary role and an *allowance*?'

Was the woman a complete fool? Or simply too forgiving? The latter possibility incensed him. Forgiveness had to be earned, and some deeds didn't deserve forgiveness. Some people didn't deserve forgiveness. Ramon knew that better than most.

She crossed her arms. 'My father can't disappear from the club altogether. It will raise questions. At worst, suspicion. For appearance's sake, he needs to maintain a presence, show his face occasionally.'

He gave her an assessing look. 'So this is about the club. Not your father?'

'Of course. The Royce needs stability. That's all I care about right now.'

He nearly bought the act, but her tone was too lofty, her body language defensive. The idea of Emily caring about her father's welfare after he'd risked her livelihood only deepened Ramon's anger. Royce didn't deserve his daughter's lenience.

Yet she made a good point. The stability of the club and its membership was paramount.

Abruptly, he said, 'An honorary position. No allowance.'

She pressed her lips together.

When she didn't respond after a moment he warned quietly, 'You need this deal, Emily.'

*As did he.*

She blew out a breath and closed her eyes. Finally, she looked at him again. 'Fine. Unless you have any more surprises to spring?'

He thought about the accountant and decided the issue could wait. 'No.'

To which she nodded wordlessly and strode from the room, giving him a very wide berth, he noted.

# CHAPTER FOUR

THE DOCUMENT FORMALISING the sale of Maxwell Royce's fifty per cent shareholding in The Royce and a further one per cent of Emily Royce's shares to the Vega Corporation was signed by all three parties at six twenty p.m. on Tuesday night.

It would have happened sooner, but Maxwell had taken almost two hours to reappear after Emily had called him on his mobile to summon him back.

He hadn't been inebriated when he'd showed but the whisky fumes on his breath had been unmistakable. Ramon had snagged her eye as they'd congregated in the boardroom and she'd known from his hard expression that he too had detected the whiff of alcohol.

Emily's heart had pounded as she'd signed her name to the agreement, and once the deed had been done she'd escaped as quickly as she could.

Except Maxwell had followed her out of the room, and when he'd called her name it'd felt wrong to ignore him.

'The honorary role…' he'd said, examining his shoes. 'I don't know what to say.'

'"Thank you" will suffice,' she'd told him, mentally shredding the little vignette she'd created in her head—the one in which Maxwell wrapped his arms around her and expressed his gratitude with a hug.

*Stupid, stupid girl.*

When had her father ever hugged her?

She had turned her back on him then and walked away and now, a day later, that small act of rejection felt petty and mean.

A knock at the office door drew her gaze away from the

window. She swivelled her chair around and glanced un-
happily at the papers strewn across her desk. She'd arrived
into the office at seven a.m. and in the two hours since then
had achieved precisely nothing.

'Come in,' she called, then wished she hadn't, when the
man responsible for her lack of productivity opened the
door and strode in.

She wanted to hate Ramon de la Vega in that moment.
As much as she wanted to hate the uncontrollable way her
body reacted to him. Just his presence had the ability to
make her feel hot and unsettled, restless, in a way she'd
never experienced before.

He closed the door and she curled her hands over the
arms of her chair.

She wished she didn't know how hard and lean he was
underneath his swanky designer suit. But after yesterday,
when she'd stumbled in her haste to back away from him
and he'd caught her, she knew there wasn't an ounce of ex-
cess fat on his powerful frame. Every impressive inch of
him was hard, masculine muscle.

She pressed her thighs together, remembering the alarm-
ing flare of heat she'd felt between her legs, the tiny thrill
of illicit excitement when his mouth had descended towards
hers. The avalanche of sensations had been so unexpected,
so different from the revulsion Carl Skinner had evoked,
she'd barely returned to her senses in time to command
Ramon to stop.

She still reeled from the encounter. He'd almost kissed
her and for one crazy, reckless moment she'd wanted him
to. Had wanted to know how his mouth would feel against
hers and if he tasted the same as he smelled…earthy, with
a hint of spice and an undertone of sin…

Emily had tried hard to forget everything about that
moment, but not even last night's frenzied baking session
or the double helping of dark chocolate mousse cake she'd

devoured had helped. Afterwards, feeling slightly ill, she'd glared at the partly eaten cake as if it had failed her somehow. Baking treats in her kitchen and indulging her sweet tooth were her favourite forms of stress release, but last night neither had brought her comfort beyond the temporary sugar hit.

'Good morning,' he said, his deep voice, with its interesting mix of Spanish and American accents, as rich and decadent as the cake she'd gorged on last night.

He smiled and she ignored the way it made her stomach flutter. Reminded herself he was the kind of man who used his looks to flatter and seduce. It wouldn't surprise her if he practised that smile in front of the mirror every morning.

She said a brisk, 'Good morning,' then glanced at her watch. 'You're half an hour early.'

Last night, before leaving, she'd suggested an introductory meeting with the department heads at nine-thirty, followed by a tour of the club and, if he was interested, some one-on-one time with each manager for an overview of their respective areas.

It had only just gone nine.

Without asking, he took a seat on the other side of her desk—the same chair Skinner had sat in two days earlier—and scanned the room. 'You have a nice office,' he said, ignoring her comment about the time.

'Thank you,' she said, because her office *was* nice, and she liked it. It'd been her father's until her grandfather had died and Maxwell had taken the larger office further up the hall. After moving in, Emily had hung a piece of colourful artwork and applied a few feminine touches to the decor. The result was a professional but comfortable space that at times felt like a second home. 'I hope it remains that way.'

He raised an eyebrow. 'Nice?'

'Mine,' she said, and his dark brows angled into a frown.

'Your job is secure, Emily.'

Emily wanted to believe him, but having faith in people had never been her strong suit, and the last few days had tested her capacity for trust. She straightened a sheaf of papers on her desk. 'I've confirmed the meeting with the department heads for nine-thirty,' she told him, moving the conversation along so she could hasten his departure from her office. 'Is there something you need before then?'

He paused for a beat, his toffee-coloured eyes remaining serious, and a thread of tension pulled at Emily's insides.

'I need you to fire your accountant,' he said.

She went completely still. 'Excuse me?'

'Jeremy Turner.'

Feeling a flicker of something close to anger, she snapped, 'I know my accountant's name. What I don't know is why you're telling me to fire him.'

'He's a liability.'

She stiffened, everything in her rejecting that statement. 'Jeremy has been with The Royce for more than thirteen years. I trust him implicitly.'

'That's a mistake.'

The certainty in his voice sent a prickle of unease down her spine. 'How would you know that?'

'I know that Jeremy Turner got drunk in a cocktail bar several weeks ago and talked to someone about your father's financial problems.'

Shock stole the air from her lungs for a moment. Jeremy had been drunk? Had been talking about her father's private affairs *in a bar*? Divulging information she had shared with him in confidence? She leaned back. Her hands shook and she fisted them in her lap. 'To whom?'

'It doesn't matter.'

'It does to me.'

Ramon expelled a breath. 'To a woman with whom I'm acquainted.'

*Acquainted? As in, lovers?* For some reason the idea

turned the taste in her mouth bitter and she promptly redirected her thoughts. She tried to think of a reason Ramon would fabricate such an allegation and drew a blank. He had no reason to lie, and she had to admit it did make a horrible kind of sense. Why else would he have suddenly set his sights on The Royce, if not because he knew they were vulnerable?

A sense of betrayal knifed under Emily's ribs. She hadn't socialised with Jeremy beyond the occasional work-day lunch, but for the last few years she'd considered him a close colleague. A confidante, of sorts.

She rubbed her forehead. 'I'll talk to him.'

'No.' The hard edge in Ramon's voice brought her gaze sharply back to his. 'Turner goes,' he said. 'No compromise.'

Even as she nursed a sense of hurt over Jeremy's misdeed, Emily balked at such a merciless stance. 'He has a right to put his side of the story forward, surely?'

'It's irrelevant.'

'He exercised poor judgement—'

'He shared personal information about his employer with a stranger. That's indefensible.'

Jaw flexing, Ramon stood, the ruthless businessman emerging from behind the easy charm. The glimpse of arrogant intractability should have repelled her. Instead her pulse quickened, her heart pumping faster.

'I need to be able to trust the people who work for me,' he added. 'As should you. There's no room for soft hearts in business, Emily. Not everyone deserves a second chance.' There was a quiet ferocity in his voice that suggested he truly believed it. 'Cut him loose,' he finished. 'Or I will.'

His ultimatum delivered, he turned and walked out before she could articulate a protest.

Emily dropped her head in her hands.

She'd awoken this morning grimly resigned to yesterday's outcome and consoled herself with the thought that at least this week couldn't get any worse.

She laughed bitterly.

*More fool her.*


Emily didn't have to fire Jeremy in the end.

He resigned.

As soon as she walked into his office and confronted him, his face crumpled with guilt and he tendered his resignation with immediate effect.

Regret made her chest ache, but Jeremy's confession had tied her hands—made it impossible for her to plead his case with Ramon.

And, though it pained her to admit it, maybe Ramon was right. Maybe she was too soft. Too forgiving. How many times had she dug her father out of trouble, only for him to disappoint her and mess up again?

She paused outside his office. Or was it Ramon's now? She'd hoped it might be hers one day, but the future unfolding was very different from the one she had imagined. Was he even in there? She hadn't seen him since the meeting with the department heads and it was after three o'clock now. She took a deep breath, knocked twice and opened the door.

He looked up from behind the big mahogany desk that used to be her grandfather's.

So he had settled in.

The knot of resentment in Emily's stomach hardened. He looked perfectly at home, as if he had every right to be there, and she hated that he did.

She closed the door and he leaned back in the enormous leather chair as she crossed the office. He'd removed his suit jacket and tie—a liberty acceptable only in the privacy of the offices, given the strict formal dress code of the club—and he looked good in just a shirt, the tailored fit of the white fabric emphasising the breadth of his shoulders and a strong, well-proportioned physique that looked more suited to a rugby pitch than the office.

She stopped in front of the desk, squeezed all inappropriate thoughts of his body out of her head and placed her hand on a chair back for support. 'Jeremy's gone,' she said, intending to sound matter-of-fact, but to her horror a faint quaver hijacked her voice.

Ramon's eyes narrowed, telling her he hadn't missed it. He studied her until heat crawled around the back of her neck. 'Sit down,' he said.

'No. I only came to tell you—'

'Sit down, Emily,' he repeated, more firmly this time, and she closed her mouth and sat, even as she scorned herself for being so meek.

Rising, he turned to a shelf on the large bookcase behind him and picked up two crystal tumblers in one hand and a heavy vintage decanter in the other. He set the tumblers on the desk. 'First time firing someone?'

She watched him pull the stopper from the decanter and pour a shot of her father's whisky into each glass. 'I didn't fire him,' she said. 'He resigned.' But she knew that was just semantics. If Jeremy hadn't offered his resignation, she'd have been forced to terminate his employment.

Ramon slid one of the tumblers across to her.

'Why are we drinking?'

'Because you look as if you need it.'

She glanced at him sharply. Was he offering comfort? Or attempting to avert what he thought might be an emotional crisis?

Grabbing the tumbler, she swallowed the whisky and winced as it burned on the way down.

'Better?' he asked after a moment.

'Not really.' Although the warmth spreading through her stomach had a rather soothing effect. She met his gaze.

His eyes reminded her of hot, molten caramel—rich and tempting, but dangerous if you dipped your finger in too soon. She cleared her throat. 'I suppose you've fired plenty of people.'

'Three.' He sat, knocked back his whisky and put the glass down. 'Trust me, it's not something that brings me pleasure.'

So they had that in common at least. His words from this morning came back to her.

*Not everyone deserves a second chance.*

Did that harsh belief stem from personal experience?

'Emily.'

With a start, she realised he had spoken. 'I'm sorry?'

'I said you have a good team here,' he said. 'Dedicated. Professional. And they respect you.'

Warmth spread through her chest, though she told herself that was from the whisky, not his unexpected praise. 'Thank you,' she said. 'They're all extremely dedicated. Most of them have been here since my grandfather's time.'

And Emily had worked hard to earn their respect. She was young, but in the three years before her grandfather's death she had worked at ground level in every department including the kitchens to prove she was serious about learning the business. No one had been able to accuse her of looking for a free ride because her surname was Royce. Even her grandfather, who had rarely given praise, had remarked on her commitment. Of course, he had gone on to say her commitment to hard work would stand her in good stead for marriage and motherhood. In his mind, her greatest obligation to the family was to provide him with at least one great-grandson who would one day inherit his precious club and his wealth. He'd even rewritten his will in a sly effort to influence that outcome.

It'd been a wasted effort, of course. Emily had no intention of being ruled by a clause in a will.

Ramon spoke again and she tried to focus. What was wrong with her? One shot of whisky and her mind was all over the place. Or was it the effect of the man sitting opposite?

'My CFO will have one of his team pick up the slack until you've recruited a new accountant.'

'Oh…' She nodded slowly. 'Okay. Thank you.'

'I have a contact at a top recruitment firm here in London,' he said. 'I'll email his details to you. Once you start the process, keep me updated.'

Feeling off-kilter and not sure why, she simply nodded. 'All right.'

'And keep Friday night free for dinner.'

'Fine—' *Wait.* 'What?' she said.

'Dinner,' he repeated.

She blinked at him. 'With whom?'

'With me,' he said smoothly.

Emily opened her mouth and closed it again.

'Is that a problem?'

*Yes.* For too many reasons to list, not least of which was that she was smart enough to know she was out of her depth with this man. He had more sex appeal than anyone she'd ever met. Dealing with him in a professional setting required every ounce of composure she possessed. Outside of the office, she wouldn't stand a chance of remaining immune.

'I thought you'd be going back to New York by the end of the week,' she said.

He gave a slow smile that made her shift in the chair. 'Eager to be rid of me, Emily?'

'Of course not.' But a hot, incriminating blush burned her cheeks. 'I'm aware you have businesses all over the world, that's all. I assume you don't stay in one place for long.'

'Not unless something holds my interest.'

The heat in her face spread down her neck. He was talking about women. She didn't know how she knew that, she just did. Maybe it was the look in his eyes—the gleam that was making her feel as if *she* were the current object of his interest. Which was, she reminded herself, how every playboy operated. They were automatically programmed to flirt. To pull out their charm like a magic wand and zap a woman's defences. It was why men like Ramon—and her father—were never short of female companionship. Not that she'd seen her father in action with the ladies for herself. But the string of glittering, vacuous women who'd come and gone over the years spoke for itself.

'I'm not sure dinner is a good idea.' She shifted again, her skin feeling sticky under her blouse. 'Yesterday…' She trailed off, waiting awkwardly for him to catch her drift.

His brows rose. 'Yesterday…what?'

At the gleam in his eyes, she pressed her lips together. *He knew what.* She glared at him, her face growing hotter. 'You almost kissed me.'

As soon as the words came out she wished they hadn't. Mentioning it gave the impression she'd been thinking about it and that would only feed his ego. Of course, she *had* been thinking about it, which made everything—this conversation included—ten times more excruciating. She wanted to groan. How had they gone from the serious topic of firing people to this?

Unlike her, Ramon didn't appear at all discomfited. 'Which is why we should have dinner.'

She frowned. 'I don't understand.'

'We're business partners now.' His tone was patient. 'We have a relationship—'

'A professional one,' she cut in.

'Yes. Which would benefit from putting the tension—and events—of the last two days behind us and starting with a clean slate.'

Meaning, he wouldn't try to kiss her again? The thought provoked a sinking sensation she couldn't explain. Ignoring it, she raised her chin in challenge. 'By having dinner?'

He shrugged. 'It's a good way to relax and talk. To get to know one another.'

Put like that, it didn't sound completely unreasonable. But caution kept her wary. 'We can talk here. In the office.'

'Or we can enjoy a meal without work-day interruptions and you can give me an opportunity to show you one of my clubs.' His lips curved in a half-smile. 'Perhaps even improve your opinion of them.'

That made her pause—from guilt as much as anything. She'd not been very complimentary about his clubs.

In truth, she was intrigued.

His properties had a reputation for unrivalled luxury, and she'd read that A-list celebrities booked up to a year in advance to hold their private soirees in his West End club. His latest venture, in Paris, was meant to be even more glamorous and exclusive.

She puffed out a breath. She'd run out of arguments, or at least any that were valid. Telling him she couldn't have dinner with him because he made her feel hot and bothered was hardly an option. She stood up. 'Fine. A *business* dinner,' she said, putting a clear emphasis on 'business'.

One evening. She could grit her teeth and bear it, couldn't she? And, when it was over, he would disappear, to New York or Spain or Dubai or wherever, and Emily would get on with doing what she did best.

Running The Royce.

Two days later, standing in her bathroom, Emily applied a final coat of mascara to her lashes, stepped back from the mirror and gave her reflection a critical once-over.

She couldn't remember the last time she'd devoted this much effort to her appearance.

She smoothed the front of her dress with both hands. It was a safe choice. The scooped neckline revealed only a hint of cleavage and the hem stopped just above her knees. The midnight-blue fabric clung softly to her body and the subtle shimmer woven through it kept it from being boring. It was classy enough for an exclusive venue, but not attention-seeking.

She uncapped a tube of tinted gloss and slicked it over her lips. She'd gone for more make-up than usual, enhancing her grey eyes with soft, smoky colours, and lightly rouging her cheeks.

Recapping the gloss, she looked at her hair and felt a stab of uncertainty. Her curls were shiny, well-conditioned, but they were thick and unruly. She should have left them in the neat chignon she'd worn to work.

She pulled open a drawer filled with hair clips and bands as her doorbell chimed from the hallway.

With a fresh bout of nerves making her hands unsteady, she glanced at her watch.

Six-fifty p.m.

*He was ten minutes early.*

And standing at the front door of her flat, she thought with a flash of unaccountable panic.

Quickly, she slipped her bare feet into a pair of high-heeled navy sandals and went to the door.

Her renovated flat was on the top floor of a converted three-storey Victorian mansion. She had told Ramon to text her when he arrived and she would meet him on the street. She paused by the hall table and checked her phone. No message.

Maybe a neighbour was calling and it wasn't Ramon. How would he have gained access? Unless Mr Johnson, her elderly ground-floor neighbour, had forgotten to lock the main door again.

Taking a deep breath, she calmed her spinning thoughts and opened the door.

And forgot to breathe out.

Ramon stood there and he was…

*Oh.*

He was breathtaking…tall and powerful and a bit edgy-looking, dressed entirely in black. He wore a jacket, no tie, an open-necked silk shirt and he hadn't shaved, leaving a dark five o'clock shadow on his lean jaw that served only to magnify his sex appeal. He looked relaxed, yet lethal—a heady combination that turned her knees watery and her insides hot.

She steadied herself with one hand on the door, slowly growing aware of Ramon conducting his own appraisal—of her.

His gaze travelled all the way down to her coral-tipped toes and back up to her face.

Their gazes locked and Emily couldn't misinterpret the dark, appreciative smoulder in his hooded brown eyes.

Heat saturated her skin.

This was business, she reminded herself, not an evening of pleasure, but the electrifying hum of physical awareness didn't lessen.

And then his gaze shifted to her hair, moving over the wild mass of honey-blonde curls that more often than not defied her efforts to tame them. Which was why she always, always restrained her hair in a tight chignon for work.

Wishing again that she'd left it up, she tugged the end of a thick curl. 'It's a little wild.' She sounded almost apologetic. 'I was going to put it back up. If you wait a minute—'

Ramon caught her wrist before she could turn away. 'Don't.' His voice was deep, gruff. 'Your hair is beautiful.'

Her heart gave a little jolt, as if his touch had cranked up the voltage on her awareness and fired a tiny electric charge through her body. 'Actually, it's a nightmare,' she said, brushing off the compliment and ignoring the small dart of pleasure that pierced her.

He released her, and though it was fanciful she imagined she could still feel the warm imprint of his fingers on her skin.

'I like it.' His lips curved and she wondered how many women had fallen prey to that lazy, sensual smile. 'Are you ready?'

Because it was too late to back out, she made herself nod. 'I'll just grab my bag.'

Reluctant to invite him in, she left Ramon at the door while she slipped her phone and a few other essentials into a silver clutch and grabbed the velvet wrap she'd left on her bed when choosing her outfit.

On the landing, she stopped to lock the door and glanced at Ramon. 'This wasn't necessary, you know. I told you, I could have met you at your club.'

'Are those the kind of men you normally date?'

She looked at him sharply and felt heat creep into her cheeks. It had been a long time since any man had taken her on a date. 'Excuse me?'

'The kind who are happy to let you traipse across the city alone at night?'

Hearing his sharp tone, she turned to him. 'This isn't a date.' She slipped her keys into her clutch. 'And we might be business partners, but I don't think my personal safety falls under your purview.'

She headed towards the stairs and Ramon fell into step beside her.

'Perhaps not,' he said. 'But it would be very inconvenient if something happened to you.'

She shot him a sidelong glance. His profile looked stern, but there'd been a teasing lilt to his voice.

'I'm quite capable of looking after myself.' She had,

after all, been doing it for a long time. 'Believe it or not, I'm even rather good at it.'

'Yet you live in a building that isn't secure.'

As they started down the stairs, Ramon cupped her elbow and the brush of his fingers was warm, light and not entirely unwelcome. After six years she was familiar with the carpeted stairs that led to her beloved home, but she normally navigated them in the ballet flats that lived in her work bag for the specific purpose of her week-day commute. Descending in four-inch heels felt somewhat more precarious.

'The main door is usually locked,' she defended, and made a mental note to have another word with Mr Johnson. 'My downstairs neighbour is elderly. Sometimes he disables the self-locking handle if he's bringing in more than one load of shopping then forgets to unlatch it.'

'You should have an alarmed access system with an intercom for visitors.'

In spite of herself, Emily's mouth twitched. 'This is Wimbledon. Not the Bronx.' Something occurred to her then. 'How did you know which flat to come to?' The converted mansion housed five residences, two each on the ground and middle floors, and hers taking up the entirety of the top floor.

'You mentioned you lived at the top.'

She thought for a moment. Yes. She might have—when they'd had the conversation which had started with her telling him she'd make her own transport arrangements and ended with him overriding her. Ramon de la Vega, for all his easy charm, was not a man accustomed to hearing no.

Outside, a sleek, black sedan of European design waited by the kerb with its driver sitting patiently behind the wheel. Ramon guided Emily into the back and then joined her from the other side. His big frame made the enclosed space, with its tinted windows and luxurious leather, feel disconcertingly small.

Emily tugged at the hem of her dress, which had ridden up as she'd slid onto the soft leather, and cast around for a conversation starter. 'Tell me about your club,' she said, settling on a topic that felt safe.

'The London club?'

'Of course.' Wasn't that where they were going? 'I read somewhere that the waiting list for membership is estimated at five years long.'

'At least.' His tone wasn't boastful, just straightforward, matter-of-fact. 'We have a strict limit of a thousand members at any one time.' He went on to describe a range of high-end facilities, including restaurants and bars, a health spa and a grooming salon, fitness amenities and luxury accommodation for members who lived abroad.

Emily felt a touch of envy as she listened. Ramon had a clear vision for his clubs and the freedom to pursue it. She, on the other hand, was hamstrung by a conservative membership that was allergic to the very whiff of change and anything that might be remotely perceived as bucking tradition.

A short while later, when the car stopped and the purr of the engine ceased, Emily realised she'd lost track of time as well as their whereabouts. She glanced out through the tinted window beside her, expecting to see the night-time bustle of London's vibrant West End, and stilled.

She snapped her head back around to look at Ramon. Anger vibrated in her voice when she spoke. 'You have exactly three seconds to explain why we're sitting on a runway next to a plane.'

His expression was calm. 'I'm taking you to Saphir.'

Confusion blanked her mind for a moment, then understanding crashed in.

'We're having dinner in *Paris*?'

Three things seemed to converge on Emily at once. Shock, panic and a tiny, treacherous streak of excitement.

She shook her head. 'That's crazy. I... I can't.'

'Are you afraid of flying?'

'No.'

'Then what's the problem?'

She sent him a furious look. 'The problem is that travelling to another country for dinner is...is *insane*.'

'The flight is less than an hour.'

She gripped her clutch tightly in her lap. 'I don't care. You misled me. You said we were having dinner at your club.'

'I didn't say which one.'

'Lying by omission doesn't excuse you.' She set her jaw. 'Anyway, this is all pointless. I don't have my passport.'

He reached inside his jacket and withdrew something.

Eyes widening, heart pumping hard, she snatched the passport off him and checked inside it. She looked up, incredulous. 'How on earth did you get this?' It should have been sitting in a safe in her office.

'Marsha,' he said.

Emily threw him an appalled look. 'You should be ashamed of yourself.'

No doubt he had layered on the charm in order to coerce young Marsha's help. The poor girl wouldn't have stood a chance in the path of all that concentrated testosterone.

Emily shoved the passport into her clutch, snapped it closed and stared straight ahead. She could see the back of the driver's head through the glass partition, but if he'd overheard their conversation he gave no sign. 'Take me home.'

'After dinner.'

Ramon climbed out and walked around the car to her side. When he opened the door and stared down at her, she crossed her arms and refused to budge. He waited, and the seconds ticked by until she started to feel childish. Finally, muttering a curse under her breath, she got out. 'For the record, I don't like surprises.'

'Everyone likes surprises.'

The amusement in his tone grated. 'I don't. And I still think this is crazy.'

He closed the door and she leaned against the car for support, as if it were an anchor in a choppy sea—a safe, solid object that would keep her grounded, and stop her doing something stupid. Something she might regret. Like getting on that damned plane.

'It's just dinner, Emily.'

His voice had a deep, soothing quality, but it didn't help, because it wasn't just dinner. Not for her. Not when she stood there contemplating a giant leap out of her neatly ordered comfort zone. She eyed the plane. It was a small, sleek private jet. 'Is that yours or did you charter it for the evening?'

'I bought it yesterday.'

'Very funny.'

'I'm serious.'

She turned her head to look at him. There was no mockery on his face. She looked at the plane again. A uniformed male attendant stood at the foot of the steps, patiently waiting. 'This is very…spontaneous,' she said weakly.

'That's a bad thing?'

'Yes.' She held her wrap and her clutch against her chest in a death grip. 'I'm not very good at spontaneous.'

'Try it.' His deep, sinful voice coaxed. Enticed. 'You might like it.'

She might.

*And where would that leave her?*

Already she felt a gazillion miles out of her depth with this man, but it was everything else he made her feel that terrified her.

Never had she felt so physically attracted to someone before. The one intimate relationship she'd had had left her feeling deeply discontented, believing in the end she just wasn't that into sex, but Ramon...

He made her think about sex.

She, who guarded her space and preferred not to be touched, had caught herself more than once thinking about his big hands and his beautiful mouth and how they might feel on certain parts of her body.

She forced herself away from the car.

Thoughts were just thoughts, weren't they? Harmless unless translated into action, and that wasn't going to happen. Theirs was a professional relationship and she was too sensible to breach that boundary. She wasn't controlled by her desires. Not like her father.

*It's just dinner.*

She thought of all the women who would give their eye teeth to fly in a billionaire's private jet to Paris for dinner and then straightened her shoulders. 'Let's not stand around all evening, then.' She set off towards the plane. 'I'm famished.'

# CHAPTER FIVE

RAMON HAD BEEN labelled 'reckless' from the day he'd been old enough to clamber out of his cot and send his mother and the entire household staff into a frenzied hour-long search of the house and grounds. As a fearless, rebellious child he'd become the bane of his parents' lives, unlike his brother, who'd never once defied authority or set a foot wrong.

As an adult, Ramon had learned to curb his impulses. The tabloids portrayed him as a playboy and his reputation wasn't entirely undeserved. But he didn't pursue pleasure with a careless disregard for the consequences, like some of his peers did. Risks, when taken, were calculated, impulses acted upon only if there was no potential for harm.

And he was no longer fearless. He understood the pain of loss. Understood that when you hurt people, when you took something precious from them, there were no words or actions that could undo the harm. No way of turning back the clock.

Tonight, as he took Emily's hand to help her from the limousine outside Saphir, Ramon understood something else. He understood that, for the first time in a long time, he had miscalculated.

Because he had believed he could keep his relationship with Emily professional. Had told himself that tonight was simply an elaborate attempt to break down her barriers and smooth the way for a more harmonious partnership. That, plus the opportunity to bring her to Saphir and showcase the best of his portfolio.

But he had failed to factor into his calculations the possibility that Emily would look the way she did tonight. Or that his body would end up humming with a raw, irrepressible desire he'd find impossible to quell.

He didn't want just to break down her barriers.

He wanted to rip off the dress that clung so seductively to every lush curve and dip of her body and haul her off to bed.

'Wow.'

She stood beside him, her face upturned, her gaze trained on the club's white stone entrance and the soaring, double-tiered archway bathed in subtle blue light. She'd loosened up in the last hour, maybe in part due to the champagne they'd consumed on the plane, along with canapés to tide them over, or maybe thanks to the small talk they'd settled into once her anger with him had subsided.

'Welcome to Saphir.' No sooner had he spoken than a pop of white light flashed in his periphery.

Blinking, Emily looked around, spotting the photographer a second after he did. 'Was he taking a photo of *us*?'

Ramon gestured to a security guard. 'Ignore it,' he said, guiding her inside with a hand pressed to the small of her elegant back. He nodded to the concierge as they entered the high-ceilinged granite and glass reception area. 'Security keeps the paparazzi at bay, but they're like flies. Swat one away and a dozen more appear. Unfortunately Saphir has become their new favourite haunt. This way.' He turned her down a hallway lined with contemporary art work and illuminated sculptures, many of which he'd handpicked in consultation with his designer. As they approached the restaurant, a willowy redheaded hostess whose name he couldn't remember greeted him with a deferential smile, relieved Emily of her wrap and escorted them through the restaurant's lively interior to a table in the private alcove he had specifically requested.

Emily took in their surroundings then looked out of the floor-to-ceiling window to an internal courtyard where sculptured water features and luxuriant plant life created an exotic, colourful haven. 'This is beautiful.'

Ramon signalled to the redhead, who pressed a button, and then the wall of glass beside them slid back.

A smile spread over Emily's face. 'I feel like I'm sitting in paradise!'

Her reaction was unguarded, her smile so beautiful, so real, that Ramon felt its impact like a burst of warmth in his chest. He was trying to process the feeling when a waiter materialised with menus, the champagne he'd pre-ordered and two *amuse-bouches* served in shot glasses with delicate glass spoons.

'*Foie gras*, figs and apricot,' the waiter explained. He uncorked the champagne, filled their flutes then melted away again.

After one mouthful of her *amuse-bouche*, Emily made an appreciative humming noise in her throat that Ramon was fairly sure he could feel in his groin.

'That is delicious.' She scraped the glass clean and savoured her last mouthful. 'Who's your executive chef?'

'Levi Klassen.'

Her grey eyes, which had a softer look about them tonight, rounded. 'The Dutch chef?'

'You know him?'

'I know of him. Our executive chef at The Royce speaks highly of him.'

He finished his own *amuse-bouche* and acknowledged it was exceptional. As he'd expected. He only hired the best. 'Perhaps we can have them collaborate on a menu some time.'

'Really? That would be amazing.' She turned her attention to the menu on the table. After a quick scan, she asked, 'Are the desserts on a separate menu?'

'Yes.'

'Oh.' She sounded disappointed.

He lifted an eyebrow. 'Problem?'

'I always check the desserts first.' She glanced up and must have seen the question on his face. 'So I know how much room to leave,' she elaborated.

Ramon tried to think of a time he'd taken a woman to dinner and watched her do more than pick at a lettuce leaf or a piece of white fish. He found himself smiling.

Her eyes narrowed. 'Have I amused you?'

'Surprised me,' he admitted. He caught the waiter's attention and sent the man for a dessert menu.

'Because I like to eat dessert?'

He shrugged. 'I don't often dine with women who admit to having a sweet tooth, let alone indulge it.'

'That's because supermodels live on diet pills and fresh air,' she said pertly and, given that a number of beautiful but rake-thin models had come and gone from his bed over the years, he was hard pressed to defend himself against that comment.

Fortunately, their waiter returned and saved him from having to. He sipped his champagne and watched as Emily studied the list of desserts, amusement mingling with a hot flare of curiosity. What other passions besides her sweet tooth did she hide beneath that beautiful, reserved exterior?

She put down the menu. 'Okay. I've made up my mind.'

The waiter noted their selections and then Emily settled back in her chair. 'The membership secretary put four new applications on my desk today.' She spoke quietly, her gaze fixed on her champagne, her long, slender fingers sliding idly along the delicate glass stem. 'I noted all four are board members of the Vega Corporation. I also saw that Lord Hanover has stamped his endorsement on all of them.' She glanced up, her expression difficult to read. 'How did you manage that?'

The same way he accomplished any major business win—by doing his homework, being prepared. 'In negotiations, there's a simple rule of thumb for getting what you want.'

She gave him a thoughtful look. 'Knowing what the other party wants?' she correctly guessed. She tilted her head, her magnificent honey-gold hair catching shards of reflected light from the modern chandelier above their heads. 'And Lord Hanover?' she asked. 'What does he want?'

His palms itched with a strong desire to bury his hands in those lustrous curls and explore their silken texture. He tightened his hand on his champagne glass. 'His son-in-law is chasing a major multi-billion-dollar construction contract in Saudi Arabia.'

Her gaze turned speculative. 'And...?'

'And he's hit a wall of red tape.'

'Ah. And you happen to have some connections that might smooth the way?'

He nodded, impressed. Emily was intelligent—he knew that—but she was also perceptive. Shrewd. 'My former Harvard roommate and friend to this day is a Saudi prince.'

Her eyes widened fractionally. 'Well...' After a moment, she lifted her champagne. 'Congratulations. Lord Hanover is very influential. Gaining his support is a smart move.'

He heard a trace of something in her voice. Not resentment—it was more wistful than bitter. Envy perhaps? 'Does it bother you that your shareholder status can't be revealed?'

She swallowed a mouthful of champagne and shrugged. 'Not really. It's just the way things are. There'd be an uproar if it was.'

'How can you be certain?'

She put her glass down. 'Because two years ago, three of our members proposed that women be permitted to join the club. It went to a ballot but things got very heated beforehand and some members threatened to leave if the proposal passed. It didn't...obviously.' She arched an eyebrow.

'That was their response to the idea of women joining their club. Can you imagine the reaction if they knew a woman *owned* their club?'

'And the proposers?'

'Ostracised. All three left within six months.'

It was outrageous but not surprising. Lord Hanover and his peers were prominent in the club and chauvinism was still rampant in their ranks. Ramon could imagine which way their votes had gone. 'So why did your grandfather leave half the business to you?' he asked. 'He must have known it could risk the club's stability.'

She took a moment to answer. 'Because my father has always been the way he is. Addicted to the high life, less so to responsibility. I guess my grandfather didn't trust his own son.'

'But he trusted you?'

Another shrug. 'He knew I was sensible. Devoted enough to do whatever was best for The Royce.'

'Including keeping your ownership secret.'

'Yes.'

So her grandfather had taken a calculated risk. Ramon could appreciate that strategy. And yet the old man had placed a tremendous burden on his granddaughter's shoulders. 'Surely people…the members…would expect that you'd eventually inherit the club from your father anyway?'

'Not necessarily. My father was only forty-six when his father died—fifty-three now. He could still remarry, have other children…other legitimate heirs.'

'Was that what your grandfather expected?'

'I think my grandfather stopped having expectations of my father a long time ago.'

'And you?'

She frowned. 'What do you mean?'

'What expectations did he have of you?'

Her lips twisted. 'My grandfather expected me to marry and start popping out babies—preferably boys—before the age of thirty. He only ever intended my ownership of The Royce to be a short-term guardianship.' She blinked and her mouth suddenly compressed in a tight line, as if she'd said more than she'd intended to and regretted the lapse. She shifted in her chair. 'I'm sure he turned in his grave many times this past week.'

'You think you've let your grandfather down?'

Her expression was tight. 'No offence, but the Vega Corporation owning fifty-one per cent of his precious club is not an outcome he would have endorsed.'

Ramon frowned. 'Would he have considered the alternative less desirable?'

Her gaze met his then slid away. 'Of course.'

'So the only person at fault is your father,' he said, but she looked unconvinced, and he wanted to reach across the table, grab her by the shoulders and give her a good shake. Either that, or drag her onto his lap and kiss the anguish from her face.

The latter held infinitely more appeal.

Her gaze came back to his, held for a moment, and awareness thickened the air between them. He saw the flicker of her eyelids, the surge of tell-tale colour in her cheeks, and knew she was just as conscious of their chemistry as he. Heat skated through him, but then the waiter arrived with their starters and Emily dropped her gaze. Lingering by the table, the waiter began to explain the different culinary elements on their plates. Ramon went to wave him off until he noticed that Emily was listening intently. He sat back and let the Frenchman finish, then watched her pick up her knife and fork and take a sample, sliding a sliver of beef carpaccio into her mouth. 'You're a foodie,' he observed, forcing his gaze away from those soft, perfectly shaped lips.

She glanced up. 'If that means I appreciate good food, then yes, I suppose I am.'

He picked up his own cutlery. 'Do you dine out often?'

She shook her head. 'Only occasionally.'

Her answer pleased Ramon more than it should have. He'd already learned from young Marsha—who had a talkative streak he'd shamelessly exploited—that Emily had no significant other and preferred working to socialising. But, workaholic or not, Emily Royce was too beautiful to escape male notice. If she'd said yes to his question, he would've imagined her being wined and dined by men with a great deal more than food on their minds, and that was sufficient to turn his thoughts inexplicably dark.

'I suppose you eat out all the time,' she said, 'With all the travelling that you do.'

'When the mood takes me.' Which, admittedly, was often. Dining alone rarely appealed and, no matter where in the world he was, he never wanted for a willing companion. Lately, however, his palate had become jaded, the abundance of food, wine and women failing to distract him.

This past week in London was a prime example. Twice he'd gone out with his friend Christophe only to return to his suite before midnight, alone. Not that he'd encountered a shortage of enthusiastic women, but none had held his interest. It'd left him restless and frustrated. Pursuing pleasure was a means of distraction. The alternative—boredom—was dangerous. It invited reflection, and looking too deeply inside himself never revealed anything good. That was why he never stood still for long. Why he always looked for his next challenge, whether in the boardroom or the bedroom.

Refocusing, he took a mouthful of rare, tender venison and, following Emily's lead, paused for a moment to savour the flavour and texture of the food. It was, he appreciated as he swallowed, outstanding.

'Good?'

Realising he'd closed his eyes, he opened them and looked straight into Emily's. 'Exceptional,' he said, dropping his gaze to her mouth, knowing he'd give up the rest of his meal in a flash for one taste of those luscious lips. There would be no boredom with Emily, he decided. Not with all those hidden depths to explore. She would challenge him in bed, just as she did in the office. Lust churned through his veins, hot and savage, triggering a flood of explicit thoughts as tempting as they were dangerous.

'May I ask what percentage of your revenue is generated by your food and beverage department?'

He looked at her, her question making a mockery of the desire raging through his body. She was talking business while he pictured her naked and spread beneath him. He wondered if he'd misread the signs of attraction and then he saw how tightly she gripped the handles of her cutlery. How short and shallow her breaths were and how the pulse in her throat flickered visibly. No. He hadn't misread anything. She was fighting for control of her body, just as he was doing. With brutal determination, he concentrated his thoughts and came up with a number that sounded correct.

And then she asked another question, something about the occupancy rate of Saphir's suites, and he understood that she was attempting to keep things impersonal. Preventing the undercurrent of sexual tension from pulling them under.

Right then his body wanted anything *but* impersonal. And yet his brain conceded that restraint was the wisest action. Emily didn't strike him as the kind of woman who indulged in casual affairs. If they slept together, and her expectations went beyond the physical side of things, she'd only end up disappointed. Or, worse, hurt.

Still, keeping his mind focused and his urges restrained proved a challenge throughout the rest of their meal. When Emily's dessert finally came, he sat with his double-shot espresso in front of him and watched her devour every last morsel of the rich, decadent dark chocolate soufflé. At the end she licked her spoon clean, the tip of her pink tongue catching one last smear of chocolate, and Ramon suppressed a groan. He could feel his body responding. Feel a stirring of the old, impulsive recklessness he knew better than to indulge.

Emily looked up and froze, the spoon in her hand suspended halfway between her mouth and the plate. 'Ramon...'

Hearing her say his forename for the first time—and in that husky, slightly breathless tone—sent a small shock-wave of heat through him that mingled explosively with the lust. He dragged his gaze from her mouth and locked onto those silver-grey eyes.

'Stop,' she whispered, her eyes wide and pleading, and he didn't feign innocence.

There was no point.

He knew his desire was stamped on his face and he wouldn't pretend it didn't exist. His reputation as a player was well-earned but he didn't engage in cat-and-mouse games. When he set his sights on a woman he pursued her without pretence. He wouldn't deny the truth, to Emily or to himself.

And the truth was, he wanted her.

She'd had too much champagne.

Emily put down her spoon and lowered her gaze from Ramon's. She couldn't watch his eyes stare at her mouth a moment longer. Not because she felt scandalised by the brazen interest in his heavy-lidded gaze, but rather because of the wild curiosity pulsing through her. The shocking temptation to lean across the table, part her lips and invite him to take what he wanted in spite of having just now implored him to *stop*.

Oh, yes. She'd had too much to drink.

And it was time to be sensible. Time to steer the conversation back to safer ground.

Except she'd tried that, hadn't she? And it hadn't worked. Worse, now she found herself not wanting to behave sensibly at all. Not yet, at any rate. She was dining in Paris in plush, exotic surroundings with a man who made her think about sex! She was, quite literally, miles removed from her normal, familiar world and she didn't feel like herself. She felt like Cinderella, and she wasn't ready for the ball to end.

She lifted her lashes and looked at him. 'Show me your club,' she said before good sense prevailed and spoiled her fun. What harm could prolonging the evening cause? Tipsy or not, she wouldn't do anything foolish. Thinking about kissing Ramon was one thing—acting on the impulse quite another.

He held her gaze, the look in those toffee-coloured eyes dark and deliciously potent.

Warmth blossomed in her stomach. Knowing he would kiss her if she let him filled her with a heady sense of feminine power she'd never experienced before.

He pushed his empty espresso cup aside. 'What would you like to see?'

'Everything.'

His lips spread in a slow smile. 'Then everything it is.'

Their tour of Saphir took almost a full hour. The club was enormous, far more extensive than Emily had imagined and utterly, unapologetically luxurious. They started with the recreation complex, where a full-service health spa and bathhouse operated twenty-four-seven alongside a yoga studio, squash courts, a huge swimming pool and a gymnasium. Despite the late hour, a handful of men and women were sweating it out on the state-of-the-art machines and the sight of their toned, sculpted physiques made Emily uncomfortably conscious of all the calorie-laden food she'd devoured at dinner.

Even more impressive than the recreation wing were the entertainment facilities. In addition to the restaurant where they'd dined, and two other eateries, the club boasted a champagne and caviar bar, a glamorous nightclub and the gorgeous Blue Lounge with its live jazz ensemble, sophisticated cocktail menu and cerulean silk-lined walls.

Emily tried to pay attention to what Ramon was telling her but she absorbed only half of what he said. She couldn't concentrate. The champagne still fizzed in her bloodstream and the sexual awareness that had shimmered like a desert heat wave across the dinner table all evening seemed only to grow more intense. By the time they stepped into another lift to travel to yet another floor, Emily felt as if she were caught in the grip of a blistering fever—one that was burning up her mind as much as it was her body.

She couldn't stop looking at him. Couldn't stop thinking that he really was the most beautiful man she'd ever seen. His bone structure was nothing short of magnificent, his face a perfect landscape of hard, contoured angles. And his mouth…

'Emily.'

The warning in Ramon's tone only vaguely registered. She felt giddy, drunk not on champagne but on the pheromones drenching her senses, and the speed of the lift shooting them skywards wasn't helping. She stumbled forward, and she couldn't honestly say if she'd done so by accident or on purpose. Ramon caught her, just as he had that day in her father's office, but this time she was prepared for the impact of hard muscle, the swathe of masculine heat, that instantly engulfed her. Their gazes tangled for breathless seconds, and when the lift doors whispered open neither of them moved.

'Are we getting out?' Her voice was husky. Alien. Not at all her own.

The doors started to close and Ramon reached his hand out to halt them, his other hand remaining on her hip. 'That's your call.'

'Why mine?'

'Because this is the penthouse.'

She blinked. The feverishness in her blood made the act of thinking a challenge. Or maybe it was the intimate press of her curves against his hard body, the hot imprint of his hand on her hip, that scrambled her brain. 'The penthouse?'

'A private suite.'

His gaze probed and she needed only a second to interpret the question blazing in his eyes. Only a second longer for the curiosity she'd failed to stem to flare brighter, wilder, in her veins. If she waited one more second, sanity would intervene and she'd be saved. Saved from doing something foolish, reckless and totally out of character.

And then she'd go home to London and never know how it felt to be kissed by a man as beautiful as Ramon.

She didn't wait. She rose up on tiptoes, the sweet lure of anticipation combined with a surge of heart-pounding adrenalin giving her the courage she needed to press her lips to his.

Her first impression was of warmth. Her second, of how firm and perfect his lips felt against hers. She pressed harder, heard a rough sound like a harsh, stifled exclamation climb his throat, and then his mouth opened over hers and suddenly they were kissing, really kissing and... *Lord.* It was everything she'd imagined and more. Passionate. Molten. Consuming.

One strong arm looped around her waist and suddenly her feet floated off the floor. Their mouths still fused, he walked them out of the lift. When her toes touched the floor again and his mouth slid off hers, a sound that was half-protest, half-plea fell from her parted lips. She opened her eyes and got a fleeting impression of plush surroundings and muted lighting before her gaze centred on Ramon. His other arm came around her, encircling her fully as he dragged her close, and she didn't flinch. Didn't try to escape despite the unfamiliarity of being held.

His gaze roved her face, settled on her mouth. 'Do you know how long I've thought about doing that?'

She stared up at him. Her lips tingled, aching for the return of his. 'Since Tuesday?'

He shook his head, one corner of his sexy mouth lifting. 'The first time we met.' He tugged her closer and coils of heat kindled in her belly. 'You were so cool. So superior.' He lifted a hand and brushed the pad of his thumb over her lower lip. 'I wanted to kiss the prim, haughty smile you gave me right off your beautiful face.'

Somehow, through the thick haze of desire shrouding her senses, her mind summoned a sliver of indignation. 'And I wanted to slap yours.'

He laughed, unabashed, and then as swiftly as it had arisen his amusement vanished and the dark, smouldering look that made her stomach swoop was back. He removed her clutch from her hand, her wrap from over her forearm, and dropped the items onto a sleek, red lounge chair. His jacket followed and then he returned to stand before her.

Heart racing, Emily pressed her palm to the centre of his chest. When she spoke her voice belonged to someone else. Someone she didn't recognise. 'What happens in Paris stays in Paris.'

Another of those slow, sensual smiles slanted his mouth. 'As the lady wishes,' he murmured, and wrapped his fingers around her wrist. He raised her hand to his mouth, kissed her knuckles then turned her palm up and bit the base of her thumb.

Emily's breath caught on a soft gasp. The sharp press

of his teeth followed by the velvet slide of his tongue was unexpected—and surprisingly erotic. Her spine loosened, her legs went weak, and then he was scooping her into his arms, holding her effortlessly against his broad chest, as he strode through the suite. Seconds later he set her feet down and she barely had time to register they were in a bedroom before he was kissing her again, the heat of his mouth on hers even more explosively potent than before. Wantonly, she slid her arms around his neck and revelled in the earthy scent of him, the hot, bold stroke of his tongue against hers and the branding heat of his palms through her dress as they took possession of her hips.

His hands slid downwards, cupped her buttocks, and a low groan rumbled up his throat. He pulled her against him hard, pelvis to pelvis, giving Emily her first taste of the sheer strength and size of his erection. Before she could acknowledge the dart of apprehension in her stomach, his fingers hooked into the soft, clingy fabric of her dress and tugged upwards. 'Lift your arms,' he commanded against her mouth.

Willingly she obeyed, stretching her arms above her head, and he dispensed with the dress with a speed and ease that suggested he was well-versed in the art of removing women's clothing—a thought Emily refused to dwell upon as she stood before him in nothing but her heels, her cream satin underwear and her pearl necklace. She reached for him, partly to disguise her self-consciousness, and partly because she craved the return of his heated body against hers.

But he took a step back. 'Patience, *mi belleza*,' he said throatily, his accent more pronounced now, and she dropped her arms helplessly back to her sides. His gaze trailed over her. Hot. Intense. 'I have seen you naked in my mind many times,' he said. 'I want to know if my imagination did you justice.' He started to move, walking around her in a slow, deliberate circle, his unhurried appraisal of her near-naked body setting fire to every inch of her exposed flesh.

Her legs trembled, barely supporting her. She closed her eyes. 'Ramon...'

'I like hearing you say my name.' His voice came from behind her and she felt the silk of his shirt brush her shoulder blades. Still he didn't touch her. 'Say it again.'

She swallowed. 'Ramon.'

'Yes, Emily?'

Excitement made her heart pound, the tension and build-up of anticipation proving unbearably sexy.

Without warning he drove his hands into her hair, his fingers spearing deep and tangling in the mass of soft curls. He tugged her head back against his shoulder and put his mouth against her ear. 'What do you want?' he rasped.

'I want you to touch me.'

'Where?' His voice was rough, laced with satisfaction and a dark note of carnality that made her insides quiver.

'Everywhere,' she whispered, and felt a deep shudder move through him.

His hands came around her waist and just the hot slide of his palms across her naked midriff triggered a rush of liquid heat between her legs. He pressed an open-mouthed kiss to her bare shoulder and she arched her back, her breasts aching with an instinctive need that he answered by cupping his hands under them and dragging his thumbs over their tips.

She moaned, luxuriating in the sensations his touch was evoking. But she wanted more. She wanted skin against skin. Blindly, she grabbed at the straps of her bra and yanked them down, knocking his hands away in the process.

'*Sí, mi belleza.*' His voice rumbled with approval. 'That's right. Show me what you want.'

She did. She seized his hands and moulded them to her

bare breasts, her back arching again as he rolled her hardened nipples between his thumbs and forefingers. A little cry of pleasure escaped her, then he was kissing her neck, and she could feel his erection nudging her bottom, teasing her curiosity until she could no longer bear to stand passive. With a boldness that ordinarily would've shocked her, she reached back and palmed his groin, and even through his trousers she could feel how thick he was. How hard. *For her.*

That heady sense of feminine power surged again, throbbing in her veins like a potent aphrodisiac. 'More,' she croaked. 'I want more.'

Shifting his weight, he swung her off her feet, took three long strides and set her down on the edge of an enormous bed dressed in soft, luxurious linens. His dark gaze locked on hers, he stepped back, tugged his shirt out of his waistband and began unbuttoning it.

Her mouth filled with moisture and she stared up at him, mesmerised by the prospect of watching him strip down to nothing right in front of her.

With deft hands he peeled off his shirt and dropped it on the floor, and Emily's eyes widened.

He was utter perfection, his torso lean and chiselled, his skin like golden satin over ridges of steel. She wanted just to sit there and look at him, take the time to indulge in a leisurely inspection, as he'd done with her. But he toed off his shoes, dropped to his knees in front of her and plunged one hand into her hair, tugging her forward so that her face was close to his.

'How much more?'

She licked her lips. 'All of it.'

Eyes gleaming, he leaned in and claimed her mouth with a searing kiss that promised her she would get exactly what she'd asked for. Then his lips travelled down her throat, trailing hot, open-mouthed kisses over her sensitised skin until he reached the hard tip of her right breast.

She arched towards him before he'd even taken her nipple into his mouth. And when he did…it was exquisite, the pleasure almost unbearable. Her hands flew to his head of their own accord, her fingers streaking into the thick, dark strands of his hair, holding him to her as he mercilessly sucked her nipple into a tight, ultra-sensitive point. And then he lavished the same attention on her other breast and she dropped her head back, wondering if she might die from the blistering heat she could feel building inside her like an out-of-control inferno.

Her bra was still strung around her ribs and he unhooked it, threw it aside then pushed her back on the bed and dragged her knickers off with such efficiency, she had no time to feel hesitant or shy. But when he grasped her knees, eased them apart and lowered his head, her body tensed.

Pausing, Ramon glanced up from between her legs, hunger, heat and a clear, white-hot intent burning in his eyes. 'You wanted it all,' he reminded her thickly.

Yes…but she hadn't been thinking about oral sex. She'd never gone there before. The ex-boyfriend with whom she'd had her one, uninspiring sexual relationship had never initiated it and neither had she. And, while she was guilty of having entertained X-rated thoughts about Ramon's hands and mouth, she hadn't considered how it might feel to have his mouth on her *there*.

But, heaven help her, she wanted to know.

She relaxed her muscles, inviting him to do as he pleased, and the first stroke of his tongue elicited a shocked gasp and sent a bolt of red-hot sensation through her that made her body jerk against his mouth. With a broad hand flattened over her stomach, he anchored her to the bed and her breath seesawed on another gasp as he gently parted her with his fingers, giving his tongue deeper, more intimate access.

*Oh, God.*

She'd never known anything like it before. Had never experienced this tight, quickening sensation in her body. Had never imagined she would enjoy being pleasured in this way. He slid a finger inside her, finding a spot with his fingertip that seemed to set off an electric current deep within her core. She felt taut, tingly, as if her body were a high-voltage wire coiling tighter and tighter around his finger. He pushed deeper, flicked his tongue, and before she understood what was happening she came, every muscle in her body tensing with surprise and the sudden, unexpected eruption of pleasure.

As her limbs went from rigid to limp, she panted his name, once, twice, and he raised himself over her, his smile a study in male satisfaction. 'That's right, *dulzura*,' he murmured, tracing a line between her breasts with the tip of one finger. 'Get used to saying my name. You are going to scream it many times before we are done.'

# CHAPTER SIX

EMILY WOULD HAVE told him how cocky he sounded if her flesh wasn't already crying out again for his touch.

She'd never experienced an orgasm like that before, yet he'd coaxed her to that sensational, mind-shattering peak with seemingly little effort.

He dropped a kiss on her mouth then levered himself to his feet, unbuckled his belt and pulled his zipper down, his gaze all the while tracking her naked, climax-flushed body.

Suddenly conscious that she was sprawled on the bed like some open-legged, sacrificial offering, Emily quickly closed her thighs and clambered backwards until she encountered the pillows. For a moment she thought she saw amusement flicker over his handsome face, but then he pushed his trousers and underwear down, kicked them off and straightened.

The air deserted Emily's lungs in a rush. Ramon de la Vega was a big man in every conceivable way and, though she was inexperienced—her sexual history confined to one partner—she knew she was small down there. Tight. Her pelvic muscles clenching with just a touch of apprehension, she watched him extract a condom from the bedside drawer, tear open the foil and roll on the sheath.

He climbed onto the bed, pulled her beneath him and kissed her, and this time she took full advantage of the opportunity to touch him, sliding her hands across the smooth skin of his shoulders, over his chest with its light smattering of hair and down the hard, ridged muscles of his abdomen. Apprehension giving way to need and excitement, she reached lower, curled her hand around his hot, rigid length and felt him tense. She tightened her hold and he growled something in Spanish against her mouth.

His knee came between her legs, pushing her thighs apart, and when he disengaged her hand from his shaft and then touched her just as intimately she could tell she was slick by the way his finger easily slipped into her. He added a second finger, stretching her a little further, and she gasped as he found the same hypersensitive spot he had earlier. A moment later he withdrew his fingers and the head of his erection replaced his hand. He stilled, poised above her, eyes locked on hers. 'Say my name.'

A tiny shred of stubbornness pushed to the fore. 'Kiss me first.'

His eyes glinted, one corner of his mouth lifting in a 'two can play that game' smile. Deliberately avoiding her mouth, he kissed her neck, finding the soft, sensitive place with his tongue that made her back arch in response. Then he pushed inside her, a strong, steady thrust that went only so far before her body resisted.

'*Dios*…you're so tight.'

He pushed in a little further and she stiffened, her body demanding a moment to accustom itself to the intimate invasion. Eyes closed, she dug her hands into his shoulders and willed her internal muscles to relax.

'Emily?'

Hearing concern in his voice, she opened her eyes, looked at him and saw a stark mix of lust and uncertainty in his expression. 'It's been a long time,' she whispered and felt her cheeks redden at having revealed that small intimate truth. She shifted and drew her knees up and back, and suddenly her body yielded and he slid all the way in, so deep and so completely they both gasped aloud and shuddered.

Groaning, Ramon buried his face in her neck and ground out more words in Spanish.

And then he rode her hard, a sheen of sweat gathering

on his skin, his magnificent body rippling above hers as he drove them both towards climax with breathtaking skill.

Emily clung to him, each powerful thrust of his body into hers pushing her closer to the edge. She tried to hold on, sensing he was close, wanting him to come at the same time as her. But there was no stopping the intense burst of pleasure that hurtled her high into the stratosphere. White light splintered behind her eyelids and then she did what she'd refused to do before.

She cried out his name.

Again. And again. And again.

Ramon hit the 'end call' button on his phone and padded through to the bedroom. It was after one a.m. and, since Sleeping Beauty had appeared dead to the world, he'd decided to make some calls in the living room.

He studied her sleeping form. Emily was an outrageous bed hog and the discovery both surprised him and amused him. She was so contained most of the time, so controlled, he had assumed she would sleep in a similar fashion—either curled into a tight ball or flat on her back, hands folded neatly on her stomach. Instead, she lay sprawled across two-thirds of the mattress, her arms flung wide and her long legs half-in, half-out of the tangled covers. She was totally naked except for the silver chain and pearl that hung around her neck, and her tumble of golden curls, damp still from their shower, spilled across the pillow, begging him to bury his hands in them.

His body stirred, lust pooling with the memory of how many ways he'd enjoyed her body in the last two hours.

She'd blown his mind. Revealed a streak of passion and daring underneath her natural reserve that he'd relished exploring. Her inexperience had surprised him but pleased him too, satisfying some dark, proprietorial part of his male ego he hadn't realised existed. He'd planned to take his time with her and he had up to a point. But the second her body had accepted him, pulling him into the heart of her tight, satin heat, he'd lost control.

And then he'd lost control in the shower too. He'd carried her in with the intention of doing no more than soaping the sweat from their bodies, and instead he'd lifted her against the tiles and plunged into her, the roar of pleasure in his veins obliterating all thought until she'd whispered urgently in his ear, telling him not to come inside her. He'd withdrawn immediately, shocked that he'd forgotten to protect them—even more shocked that for one reckless, fleeting second he'd wanted to bury himself inside her again and say to hell with the risk.

He'd stood panting, torn between lust and good sense until, with a bold, saucy look that'd stopped his breath, Emily had dropped to her knees, wrapped her fingers around him and taken him in her mouth. He'd tried to summon a protest but his attempt had been half-hearted at best, and in a matter of seconds she'd brought him to the edge of completion.

Ramon had slept with countless women in countless places, but standing in that shower, with his hands braced against the walls, staring down at Emily's flushed, satisfied face, had been the single most erotic experience of his life.

Her words from earlier came back to him.

*What happens in Paris stays in Paris.*

At any other time, such an edict would have suited him down to the ground. What self-professed playboy wouldn't want to hear words that relinquished him of any unwanted strings or emotional commitments?

And relationships without strings were Ramon's golden rule. It was how he'd lived his life for the last twelve years and how he intended to carry on. Forming attachments was something he avoided for good reason. You couldn't hurt people if they didn't get close.

The thought of hurting Emily made him feel physically ill. She was tough, but he sensed her outer armour shielded an underlying vulnerability. Their conversations hadn't touched on family, but he recalled reading some tabloid bio on Maxwell that had talked of his wife having died in childbirth.

How must it feel, knowing the woman who'd given you life had lost her own while bringing you into the world? He couldn't imagine it, yet *he* knew a worse pain. The pain of knowing his actions, his choices, had led to another person's demise—not once, but twice.

His hand tightened around his phone. He had no business comparing Emily's life to his own. Unlike him, she had done nothing wrong. She wasn't responsible for her mother's death.

He thought of his mother, Elena, and her difficulties with conceiving and carrying a child to term. Having Ramon after adopting Xavier must have been quite the shock. To their credit, his parents had shown no favouritism, treating their sons with equal affection, but no doubt it'd been a great irony for them that Ramon—their own flesh and blood—was the one who'd proved a disappointment. Who had shamed the family. His mother was a good woman, but he wouldn't blame her if she never found it in her heart to forgive him.

He ran his gaze over Emily's face, wincing at the small patches of redness where his stubble had grazed her skin. He felt a tightness grip his chest. He'd known her for less than a week yet he knew she was strong and principled—a good woman, like his mother. Was that why she made allowances for her father? Or was it because she had no one else? Her grandfather was dead, she had no siblings and there didn't seem to be any extended family on the scene. Aside from Royce, who hardly qualified as a contender for Father of the Year, was Emily alone in the world?

The tightness intensified and with it came a vague sense of unease. Since when did he speculate on the personal lives of his lovers?

Yet he knew he couldn't class Emily as one of his casual flings. His relationship with her was primarily a professional one and tonight he'd crossed a line he shouldn't have crossed. He'd been reckless, allowing his base desires to govern him, and he knew he should be regretting it right now, but he wasn't. Instead, he was thinking about pulling the sheet away, easing her thighs apart and tasting her again. He was thinking that one night, a few brief hours, wasn't enough time to do all the things he wanted to do with her...*to* her. And he was thinking that, if their time together had to be confined to Paris, then perhaps this one night wasn't long enough. Perhaps they needed the whole weekend.

Her eyes opened and she blinked drowsily, stretched her gorgeous limbs and smiled up at him with lips pink and swollen from his kisses. 'Ramon?'

*'Sí, mi belleza?'*

'What time is it?'

'Late—or early, depending on your view.'

She rose onto her elbows. 'Do we need to go? Is the plane waiting for us?'

He put his phone on the nightstand. 'No. I've stood the pilot down for the night.'

A flicker of anxiety showed in her face. 'Will he be available to take us back first thing in the morning?'

Ramon climbed onto the bed. 'He's available when I want him to be available.' He pushed the tangled sheet off her and palmed the soft mound of honey-blonde curls at the apex of her thighs. Slowly, he ran a fingertip down her sensitive flesh and her soft gasp made his groin tighten. 'Tender?'

'Only a little.'

He gave a slow smile then moved his hand and made her gasp again. 'In that case, I'll be gentle.'

Bright morning sunlight streamed through the lounge windows of the penthouse and for the first time in Emily's life she truly appreciated the sentiment behind the expression 'the cold light of day'.

She pulled the belt of the fluffy white bathrobe tighter around her waist. 'No,' she said and felt an immediate rush of relief, because the other word she could have uttered— the big, fat, resounding *yes* that was even now attempting to crawl up her throat against her better judgement—could not, under any circumstances, be allowed to escape. 'I can't stay another night. I need to go home to London this morning.'

*And I need you to put some clothes on*, she almost added, although thankfully only his chest was on display. He wore his dark suit trousers from last night but they weren't belted or zipped properly and they sat too low on his hips. She knew if she let her gaze drop she'd see more of his flat, muscled stomach than her composure could handle at present.

Unaware of her internal struggles, he poured coffee from a silver pot into two china mugs. 'Is there something you need to return for today?'

'Yes,' she lied, accepting the coffee he handed her without meeting his eye. Her *sanity*. That was what she needed to return for. Because clearly she'd lost it somewhere between here and London and she could really do with getting it back before the wanton, needy creature he'd unleashed in her decided that staying in Paris with him was more appealing than returning home.

She took her coffee over to the big floor-to-ceiling window and stared out at the stunning view of the city.

Perhaps the light of day wouldn't have seemed so harsh right now if she hadn't emerged from the bedroom at just

the wrong time. If the man who'd been wheeling a heavily laden breakfast trolley out of the lift hadn't glanced at
her and she hadn't seen, in the moment before he blanked
his expression, the speculative glint in his eyes. He'd been
judging her, eyeing up the drowsy, bed-rumpled woman
who'd slept with his boss—and, given she was guilty as
charged, could she really blame the guy for looking at her
as if she were a two-bit slut?

She swallowed, self-disgust rising in her throat like bile.
She'd set aside all manner of caution and self-preservation
and let curiosity and pure physical lust take control.

*Oh, God.*

All these years of despising her father's behaviour and
now she couldn't even claim the moral high ground.

She gripped her mug between her hands. She couldn't
spend another night in Paris with Ramon. Just thinking
about the things they would do together made her skin flush
with heat and her body tremble with a deep-seated longing she couldn't quash. He was like a dangerous, addictive
narcotic. She'd had her first hit, experienced the ecstasy of
the high, and now she was craving another.

Could addiction take root so quickly?

She shook her head. Crazy thinking. She was out of her
element, her comfort zone, and she'd just done something
completely out of character. Something that—even now
with self-condemnation dragging at her stomach—had felt
wrong and yet impossibly right at the same time.

Good grief. No wonder she was feeling disoriented.

'Emily…' Ramon's arms came around her from behind
and she stiffened so suddenly her coffee spilt, the hot liquid scalding her thumb.

Cursing softly, he took the mug away and returned with
a napkin.

She patted her hand dry. 'Sorry.'

'For what? For flinching when I touched you just now, or for what we did last night?'

Hearing an edge to his voice, she fisted the napkin in her hand. What could she say? That she wasn't used to having someone put their arms around her? She wasn't. She was more comfortable when people kept their distance, though not because she didn't crave human contact. Contrary to the nasty things her ex had said after she'd ended their relationship, her veins didn't run with ice water. But when you hadn't been hugged much as a child, when you had never experienced the physical manifestation of a parent's unconditional love, you were hardly going to blossom into a touchy, feely adult.

And as for last night…her and Ramon…that hadn't been about affection, or emotion. It had been about sex.

Nothing else.

She drew a deep breath. 'I think last night was a mistake.' His eyes rapidly narrowed and she hastened to add, 'I'd had too much champagne. I… I was tipsy.'

His face darkened. 'Are you saying I took advantage of you?'

'No! Of…of course not,' she stammered, instantly regretting her feeble excuse. 'But…my judgement was impaired.' She twisted the napkin between her hands and cringed inwardly. She was making a hash of this. 'I… I wasn't thinking straight.'

'Are you drunk now?'

She blinked. 'No.'

'Are you thinking straight?'

Hardly. How could she think straight with his bare, muscled chest and powerful shoulders dominating her field of vision? 'Yes.'

Moving with lightning speed, Ramon grabbed the belt of her robe and gave it a single hard yank.

Before Emily had time to react, the sides of the garment gaped open and exposed her naked breasts.

She made a small, startled sound and tried to tug the robe closed but his arm was already snaking under the soft terry towelling and circling her waist like a band of reinforced steel.

He hauled her against him, plunged his other hand into her loose, bed-tousled curls and cupped the back of her head.

Her breasts tingled, her nipples hardening into treacherous points of need. 'Ramon—'

His mouth came down on hers. Hot. Forceful. A teensy bit brutal. Somewhere in her reeling mind she wondered if she should struggle, try to bite him, perhaps. She didn't. Instead, she curled her hands over his shoulders, arched her body like the wanton creature he'd turned her into and opened her mouth under his. He backed her against the solid glass window, his kiss growing more fervent, more demanding, and she didn't notice he'd released her head until she felt his hand sliding between her legs. A single finger thrust inside her, right into the centre of her wet, pulsing heat, and she gasped against his mouth.

He lifted his head, withdrew his finger and, holding her gaze, very deliberately put it into his mouth. He sucked, extracting his finger slowly, and then licked his lips. His smile was utterly, wickedly shameless. 'That doesn't taste like a mistake to me.'

Outrage surged, instantly tempering the hot pulse of desire between her legs.

How dared he smash through her defences and mock her in a way that was so…so *erotic*?

She banged the heels of her hands against his chest, twisted out of his grip and yanked the robe closed. 'I'm going to get dressed,' she told him, holding her chin high, injecting a hard, chilly note into her voice. 'And then I'd like to go home please.' Her throat feeling tight all of a sudden, she secured the belt around her waist and strode towards the bedroom.

'Emily.'

Civility overriding the urge to ignore him completely, she stopped and turned, just as a brown paper package bound with string landed at her feet.

'Clothes,' he supplied before she could ask. 'So you don't have to worry about the 'walk of shame'.'

He turned away to the breakfast tray and Emily stared at his back. Then she picked up the package, blinked away the sharp sting of unexpected tears and shut herself in the bedroom.

By the time the London limo driver turned into her quiet neighbourhood street, a headache pounded in Emily's temples and she felt as if her nerve endings had been wrapped in razor wire.

Ramon sat beside her on the back seat, silent and brooding, as he had been for most of the journey. They were both angry. Both upset. Which only reinforced Emily's belief that they'd made a terrible mistake. Jeopardised their professional relationship for—*what?*—a bit of short-lived gratification?

She wiped a clammy palm over her thigh. The jeans she wore fit perfectly, as did the sleeveless, pale blue top and matching cardigan. Even the underwear was the right size. Every item she'd found in the neatly wrapped package had been new, the tags still attached. Emily was appreciative but she didn't want to think too hard about whomever had bought and delivered the clothing and what they must have thought of such a task. Or maybe they hadn't thought anything. Maybe they were used to running such errands for their boss.

The idea made her feel slightly ill.

The limo stopped. Ramon said nothing, so she quietly gathered up her things.

'Are you staying in London?'

He turned his head and looked at her and electricity arced between them, as red-hot and incandescent as ever. Anger, it seemed, had only intensified their chemistry.

'No. I'm returning to New York.'

'Good.' She prayed the word sounded more convincing to his ears than hers. 'I think it would be wise if you stayed away for a while. Gave us both some…space. We can conduct any business by email and phone.'

A muscle flickered in his jaw. 'I'll come to *our* club in person whenever I deem fit.'

Stiffening at his arrogant tone, she opened her mouth to offer a pithy retort and found she had nothing. 'Goodbye, Ramon,' she said instead, ignoring the sudden dull ache beneath her breastbone, and climbed out.

He said something but Emily didn't catch it, his words muffled by the thud of the limo door as she slammed it closed.

# CHAPTER SEVEN

SIX WEEKS.

That was how long it was before Ramon finally returned to London, although it had taken considerably less time for him to conclude that his morning-after behaviour in Paris had been reprehensible.

*Abominable.*

He hadn't reacted well to rejection. Yes, Emily could have handled the situation with more grace than she had, but his own behaviour had lacked any degree of decorum. He wasn't unfamiliar with self-contempt and regret, but until that weekend those particular demons had not sat so heavily on his soul in a long time.

So he'd respected Emily's wishes and stayed away, keeping their communication to a minimum.

But six weeks was long enough. He was done with the polite, impersonal emails. The short, stilted phone calls. She still hadn't hired a replacement accountant and he wanted to know why. If she was keeping the position open in the hope that he would grant Turner a pardon and allow her to invite the man back, she was courting disappointment.

He walked down the carpeted corridor on the executive level of The Royce and saw Marsha sitting at her desk. At his approach, her eyes widened and she jumped up as if she'd been stuck with a cattle prod. 'Mr de la Vega! I didn't know we were expecting you.'

'You weren't.' He unleashed a good-humoured smile and gestured to the closed door of Emily's office. 'Is she in?'

'Er...no.'

'When will she be back?'

She blinked then stared at him.

'Marsha?' he prompted.

'I… I don't know.'

He frowned. 'What do you mean, you don't know?'

'I mean…she's not in today. She's sick…' Marsha bit her lip. 'At least, I think she's sick… She rang yesterday morning and said she was taking the day off—which is very unusual. And then today…she left a message on my phone early this morning, saying she'd be in before noon, but I haven't seen her yet.'

He glanced at his watch. 'It's after two p.m.'

Marsha wrung her hands. 'I know.'

'Have you tried calling her?' he demanded.

'Twice. I left her two messages. She hasn't called back.'

An icy sensation hollowed out his gut. That didn't sound like the dedicated, conscientious Emily Royce he knew.

'Call me if you hear from her,' he commanded and turned on his heel.


Emily opened her eyes.

Someone was pounding on her door. Or was it the pounding in her head that she hadn't been able to shake for two days that she could hear?

Her doorbell chimed, the sound piercing in the silence of her flat, and Emily groaned. It was a week day and her neighbours should all be at work, except for Mr Johnson, who was retired. But he had never climbed the stairs to visit her. Of course, he could have forgotten to lock the main entrance again, in which case the person banging on her door could be a stranger.

She groaned again, closed her eyes and snuggled deeper into the softness of the sofa.

'Emily!'

She froze, the sound of her name being barked on the other side of the door forcing its way into her stress-addled mind. She knew that voice. Deep, masculine…

'Emily!'

She sat up—too fast, apparently, because her stomach performed a sharp lurch and roll.

Ramon was at her door.

The knowledge sent a rush of heat over her skin followed closely by a cold wave of dread.

*He knows.*

She swallowed hard and fought down the flare of irrational panic with a forced dose of sanity.

*Of course he doesn't know.*

She'd only found out for herself a little over a day ago, though she'd had her suspicions for almost three weeks before visiting her doctor.

The doorbell pealed again, repeatedly, as if he were leaning on it, and she threw off the light cotton throw she'd curled under and urged her legs to move. When she opened the door a moment later, the thought came to her, much too late, that she looked a mess.

The fact that Ramon looked both powerful and sexy in his immaculate three-piece suit made her feel hot and unaccountably irritable at the same time.

She dragged her attention from his body, blotting out images in her head that she'd tried hard for the last six weeks to forget, and focused on his face. A deep frown marred his brow.

'Are you all right?'

'Yes.'

'I knocked for ages.'

'I was asleep.'

His gaze tracked over her grey tee shirt and black yoga pants then returned to her face. Her very pale, make-up-less face. 'Are you unwell?'

'Yes—no...' She shook her head. Tried to bring some semblance of order to her thoughts. 'Why are you here?'

'I went to the club,' he said. 'Marsha thought you might be sick. You haven't returned her calls.'

Confusion descended. She glanced at her watch and her heart lurched. It couldn't be almost three o'clock! It'd been only ten a.m. when she had decided to take some pain-killers and lie down for half an hour before heading into work. She'd slept for almost five hours which, now that she thought about it, wasn't all that surprising given she hadn't slept a wink during the night.

She put her hand to her forehead, guilt surging. 'Oh, no. Poor Marsha.' She turned towards the hall table where she'd left her phone. 'I need to call her.'

Not waiting for an invitation, Ramon stepped inside and closed the door. 'That can wait,' he said, taking hold of her shoulders and turning her to face him.

Emily tensed. His touch had been seared into her mem-ory ever since Paris, but memory was no match for the re-ality of having his hands on her body, even in a non-sexual way. Her heart raced and she felt warm, a little lightheaded.

His gaze scoured her face. 'Something's wrong,' he stated, his voice firm with certainty. 'What is it, Emily?'

Fear gripped her throat and for a moment she couldn't speak. Revealing her condition was something she had planned to do in her own time, when she had managed to come to terms with it herself. She'd wanted to put care-ful thought into how she would tell him, but now he was here and she no longer had that luxury. She had to tell him now, because the alternative was to lie, and she couldn't do that. Not about something so important, so potentially life-changing.

She swallowed, her throat painfully dry. 'I think you'd better come in.'

His hands dropped from her shoulders, and she knew a moment's regret, because their weight and warmth had felt oddly steadying in the midst of the tumult occurring in her body and mind.

But soon, *very* soon, he would share the tumult. And then he might not feel so inclined to offer support.

Her stomach churning, she led him through to her lounge. Like the rest of her flat, it was light and spacious, and decorated by her own hand, the palette of soft creams, pale lemons and blues intended to create an elegant, soothing space that invited one to relax. She loved this room, but she was conscious now that in less than nine months' time the cream carpet and pale colour scheme would be terribly impractical.

She stood by the sofa, thought about offering him tea or coffee—or something stronger—then decided against it. She doubted he would stay for long.

'I'm pregnant.' Saying the words out loud made her knees do a little wobble, but she stayed standing, even as a renewed bout of nausea rolled through her.

In the middle of the room, Ramon went as still as a statue, and his face... A small, detached part of her mind was fascinated by the way the colour slid right out from under his skin, leaving a pallor that made it look as if someone had tipped a bucket of whitewash over him.

Emily wrapped her arms around her middle. Waited for him to say the words she imagined most men came out with in this situation.

*Is it mine?*

The seconds ticked by in heavy silence, and she felt as if she were a character in some tacky scene from an overdramatic soap opera. The final line of dialogue had been delivered and the actors had paused for dramatic effect before the show cut to a commercial break. The random thought nearly tore a hysterical giggle from her before she caught herself. She closed her eyes. What was wrong with her? Nothing about this was funny.

'Have you confirmed it with a doctor?'

It took her a moment to realise it wasn't the question she'd expected. That he wasn't doubting that he was the father. Wasn't insulting her by suggesting there were other men to whom she could point the finger. 'Yesterday,' she said, her throat growing thick with something awfully like gratitude.

A glazed look entered his eyes and she knew he was processing. 'We used protection.'

Emily had said those same words to herself, over and over. It hadn't changed the outcome. She shrugged. 'Condoms aren't foolproof,' she offered. 'And maybe…the shower…?' Their gazes locked, the sudden, scalding intensity of his transmitting loud and clear that he hadn't forgotten the things they'd done to each other under the steaming water.

Ramon looked away, dragged his hand over his mouth and breathed in hard, his nostrils flaring. 'Give me a minute,' he said abruptly, and walked out of the room.

Emily stared after him, her breath locking in her chest as realisation struck and her stomach curled into a hard, familiar knot of resignation. Ramon was walking away, doing exactly what she'd expected him to do, exactly what she had known he would—so why was a silly sob pushing its way up her throat?

She slapped her hand over her mouth but she was too slow and the sob escaped, making a loud, choked, hiccupping sound. A *humiliating* sound.

Ramon appeared in the doorway, his brows clamped together. 'Emily?'

She jerked her hand down. 'Just go.' Somehow she managed to inject some backbone into her voice. 'I'm fine. I don't need you to stay. This is my problem to deal with.'

He stood looking at her for a long moment, then he stalked across the room and her heart surged into her throat. He looked angry but, as he drew closer, the hard lines bracketing his mouth resembled determination more than fury. He stopped in front of her, lifted his hands and framed her face. The warm pressure of his palms against her cheeks made her pulse skitter. 'I am not leaving,' he said. 'I am going downstairs to dismiss my driver and then I'm coming back here so we can talk.'

She stared at him in stunned silence.

'Do you understand me, Emily?'

Her brain told her a simple 'yes' would suffice, but her throat suddenly felt too tight to speak. So she simply nodded. And then she sank onto the sofa, watched him leave and waited for him to return.

Ramon braced his palms on the wall outside Emily's flat and sucked in one lungful of air after another.

He didn't need to go downstairs. A simple text message to his driver had done the job. But he'd needed an excuse to grab a moment alone, to get a handle on himself—on the turbulent emotions storming through him.

*Dios.*

He wanted to run. To somewhere. To anywhere. As fast and as far away as his legs would carry him.

How the hell had this happened?

*Stupid question.* He knew how it had happened. He'd been reckless. Unthinking. And now he was the father of an unborn child.

*Another* unborn child.

Another innocent life to destroy.

His breath shuddered out of him. He wasn't meant to be a father, or a husband. Husbands and fathers were supposed to protect the people close to them and Ramon had already failed that test on a spectacular scale. He kept people, his family included, at arm's length for a good reason: to protect them from *himself.*

He swallowed hard and straightened, a grim sense of determination rising in him, pushing through the turmoil, calming both his thoughts and his breathing. It was the same determination that had seen him do his family and friends a favour by walking away from them twelve years ago, except this time Ramon wouldn't be walking away. How could he? He'd been presented with an opportunity to protect his unborn child—an opportunity he'd been denied all those years ago. He'd barely processed Emily's revelation, but he had enough clarity of mind to recognise that he was being given a rare second chance. A chance to do something right…this time.

He pulled out his phone, called Marsha and told her Emily had the flu and wouldn't be back for at least two days.

When he re-entered the flat she was sitting on one end of the cream sofa where he'd left her. Her hands were clasped on her knees, her grey eyes big and unblinking. They grew even larger when she saw him as though, in spite of his assurances, she hadn't truly believed until that moment that he'd return. That she'd assumed he would desert her filled him with too many emotions to examine. He removed his suit jacket and draped it over the back of an armchair.

'It's yours,' she said.

He turned to her. 'Pardon?'

'The baby.' Her fingers fiddled with the pearl around her neck. 'It's yours.'

He sat beside her, clasped her chin and forced her gaze up when she tried to look away. 'I know.'

Her tongue came out to moisten her lips in a nervous gesture that he shouldn't have found arousing in the circumstances—but he had lain in bed and thought about those lips on many nights during the past six weeks of self-imposed celibacy, and they were just as lush and pretty as he remembered.

He dropped his hand. 'I'm sorry, Emily.'

'What for?'

'For the way I behaved in Paris. I wanted another night with you. When you refused, I didn't like it,' he confessed. 'I was out of order.'

She shrugged. 'I'm not proud of my behaviour, either. And, since we're making apologies…' colour seeped into her pale face '… I didn't sleep with you because I was drunk.'

He knew that, but the part of his male ego she'd wounded six weeks ago appreciated hearing it all the same. He lifted his hand again and traced the elegant arch of one cheekbone with his thumb. 'You look tired,' he remarked. 'And pale. Have you eaten today?'

She shook her head, her long, untethered curls tumbling about her shoulders. 'I've been a bit ill.'

'Are you drinking plenty of water?'

'Some…not as much as I should.' She stood up, her plain tee shirt and stretchy black leggings emphasising that she'd lost weight.

He frowned. Just how ill had she been?

'Actually, I could kill a cup of tea,' she said. 'I'll make us a pot.'

'Sit.' He rose to his feet. 'I'll do it.' Her eyes widened and he adopted an affronted air. 'You don't think I can make tea?' he challenged.

A faint smile crossed her features. 'I'm sure you're very capable. But it's my kitchen and I know where everything is. And I've done nothing all day… I need to move.'

He let her go without further protest, then sauntered to the window, thrust his hands in his pockets and studied the street below. He let his thoughts run to practical matters. The building wasn't wired with a security system and that bothered him. The neighbourhood seemed respectable but good neighbourhoods weren't immune to crime. The building's current security measures were flimsy and not helped by her downstairs neighbour who repeatedly left the main entry unlocked. Ramon had walked straight in today, just as he had six weeks ago.

And the stairs…three flights of them. Should pregnant women climb stairs every day?

He heard movement behind him and turned. Emily carried a wooden tray bearing a blue china teapot and matching cups. He waited for her to place the tray on the coffee table before he spoke. 'You can't stay here.'

She looked up, one hand gripping the handle of the teapot. She frowned as if he'd spouted something unintelligible. 'Excuse me?'

'Come and stay with me at Citrine.'

'Your West End club?'

'Yes. I'm using the penthouse. I can make it available for us long-term.'

Slowly, she put the teapot down and straightened. 'Why?'

'Because it's safer. And closer to work for you.' He paused. 'Not that you'll want to do that for much longer, of course.'

She stared at him. 'What are you talking about?'

He pulled his hands from his pockets and reminded himself that she was tired and stressed. Most likely not thinking straight. 'Emily,' he said patiently, walking towards her. 'Your life is about to change. Permanently. We need to consider what's best for you and the baby.'

'What's best for me,' she said, her voice rising a notch, 'is to stay in my own home.'

'It's not secure here.'

'This is a decent neighbourhood!'

He put his hands on her shoulders to calm her, but she shrugged him off and took a step back.

'Bad things happen in good neighbourhoods all the

time,' he said. 'And what about the stairs? How do you think you'll cope with those in six months' time?'

She put her palms to her cheeks. 'Ramon—just slow down for a minute. Please.'

'Emily. We need to talk about these things.'

She shook her head.

'Make some decisions,' he pressed. 'Think about the future.'

'Oh, my God.' She scrunched her eyes closed. 'Next you'll be suggesting we get married.'

Her tone was incredulous and Ramon clenched his jaw, jamming his hands back into his pockets. Marriage ranked right alongside fatherhood on his list of undesirable scenarios, but he'd be lying if he said the idea hadn't crossed his mind in the last twenty minutes.

When he remained silent, she opened her eyes and gave him a blunt look. 'I'm not marrying you.' She picked up the teapot and started pouring as if she hadn't just plunged a knife into the heart of his male pride. 'And besides…' She set the pot down and straightened again. 'Don't you think all these suggestions are a little premature? I'm only six weeks along and—' She hesitated, biting her lip for a moment, her gaze lowering. 'Miscarriages aren't uncommon in the first twelve weeks of pregnancy,' she finished quietly.

This time her words cut deeper than his pride and he felt their impact like a cold blade under his ribs. The sharp reminder of history only strengthened his resolve. 'I know,' he said, deciding then and there on a more ruthless approach. 'I've lost a child before.'

The look of shock on Emily's face was swift and complete. Her hand flew to her stomach. 'Oh, Ramon… I'm so sorry. That must've been awful.'

He picked up a cup and took a mouthful of black tea, welcoming the hit of warmth in his stomach. 'It's ancient history,' he said, replacing the cup. 'But, yes, the experience was difficult. My girlfriend miscarried and I was helpless to prevent it.' It wasn't the full story but hopefully enough to elicit Emily's sympathy. With a hand on her slender waist, he guided her to the sofa, handed her her tea as she sat and pressed home his advantage. 'You're clearly not well,' he observed. 'And you could have some challenging months ahead. Why stay here alone when there's an alternative?'

She shook her head, her jaw taking on a stubborn tilt. 'I'm fine.'

'You're pale and weak.'

'I'm in shock,' she defended. 'I haven't known about this for much longer than you have. And I have a bit of morning sickness, that's all.'

He sat down beside her. 'Your mother died in childbirth.' He delivered the words as gently as he could, but still her face drained of what little colour it possessed. Ramon himself wasn't unaffected by the statement. The thought of Emily dying evoked a dark, volatile emotion that tore through his chest.

Her hand rose to her throat and he saw her fingers tremble as they closed around the pearl. When her gaze met his, the naked appeal in her eyes reached into his gut like a fist and squeezed. 'Can we just slow this down?' she implored him. 'Take one day at a time? Please?'

He inhaled a deep breath. 'Slow' wasn't how he preferred to do things but he knew that pushing Emily too hard in her current state would be counterproductive. Which meant a change of tack was required. He expelled his breath, making a swift decision. 'Of course,' he said, then got to his feet and pulled out his phone.

She frowned. 'Who are you calling?'

'Someone who'll arrange to have my things packed and brought over.'

Her eyes rounded. 'I beg your pardon?'

'If you stay,' he said, 'then so do I.'

She stared at him and then she flopped against the sofa and slapped her hand over her forehead. 'Oh, my God.' Her laugh held a touch of hysteria. 'You're really *not* leaving.'

Calmly, he hit the number for the concierge at Citrine and put the phone to his ear.

Emily glowered at him.

He glowered back. 'Drink your tea, Emily.'

Emily awoke with a violent shiver. She felt cold. She lifted her head and saw she'd thrown the duvet and sheets off some time during the night. She'd had a hot flush, she suddenly remembered. Was that a symptom of early pregnancy? Or was it more to do with the man who was sleeping in the spare room across the hall?

She squinted at her clock. Four a.m.

Sighing, she dragged the duvet over her and stared at the ceiling. None of this felt real. The pregnancy. Ramon being in her home. A future looming that was nothing like the one she'd envisaged.

Not that she'd ever devoted much time to pondering her future beyond running The Royce. Marriage and children weren't things she'd allowed herself to dwell upon. Doing so had filled her with an unsettling yearning. A feeling of emptiness she could only banish by burying herself in work.

And there was nothing wrong with that. Nothing wrong with being a career woman. Not every girl got to marry the perfect man and have the perfect family, the perfect life. Look at her mother—she'd married a charming, handsome man who'd turned out to be a philandering pleasure-seeker and then died having his child.

A metallic taste surged in her mouth.

*Oh, no.* Was she going to be sick?

She tossed the covers off, sat up and waited for a moment to see if the nausea would pass. She should grab her robe or a sweatshirt, she thought. She and Ramon were sharing her only bathroom and she was wearing only knickers and a cotton...

She clapped her hand over her mouth, ran from her room and reached the toilet just in time.

*Ugh*. She hated this. *Hated* it.

She retched again and, as she tried to scrape her hair away from her face, felt a warm, firm hand touch her back.

Ramon didn't say a word. He just knelt behind her, relieved her hands of her hair and waited for her to finish.

'I'm done,' she croaked a long, humiliating minute later, and he helped her to her feet and gave her space to clean herself up at the basin.

When he scooped her up she acquiesced with a shameful lack of protest and, despite her mental exhaustion, she was acutely conscious of everything as he carried her back to her room. His strong, muscular arms. His clean, soapy scent. His hard, tee-shirt-covered chest under one of her hands.

She shouldn't have liked any of it.

She liked all of it.

He sat her on the edge of her bed and pressed a glass of water into her hand. 'Drink.'

'You're very bossy,' she muttered.

He crossed his arms over his chest. 'And you're very mouthy for someone who's just been hugging the toilet bowl.'

It was difficult to find a dignified response to that, so she sipped her water instead. Her throat hurt. And so did her head. Although she figured that wasn't from throwing up so much as it was a side-effect of the relentless racing of her mind over the past forty-eight hours.

She put the glass on the nightstand. Her hand trembled, but it was nothing compared to the uncontrollable shaking inside her. 'I'm not sure I can do this,' she said, fear and uncertainty crashing in like a fast-moving tidal wave she couldn't outrun.

He dropped to his haunches. 'Do what?'

'Have a baby,' she whispered.

His shoulders tensed, a stark expression descending over his features, and her heart clenched as she realised he'd misinterpreted her words. 'No,' she said hurriedly, cursing herself silently. 'I don't mean that. I don't want to get rid of this baby, Ramon.'

How could she have forgotten what he'd told her? That he had lost a child? The revelation not only shocked her but cast him in a different light. It was easy to look at Ramon and see only the confidence and charm. But he had suffered something devastating. That kind of loss had to leave a scar. She inhaled a deep breath. 'I mean… I don't know *how* I'm going to do this. I feel…'

'What?'

She shrugged, reluctant to articulate such a weak emotion. 'Scared,' she admitted, and glanced away.

Slipping a finger under her chin, he returned her gaze to his. 'I think you can do anything you set your mind to, Emily Royce.'

His tone was firm, his vote of confidence unexpected, and a burst of warmth blossomed in her chest.

But was he right?

She knew nothing about motherhood. Nothing about the bond between mother and child. She'd never had her own mother to bond with. No aunts or grandmothers or female role models. Just her strict teachers at boarding school and her grandfather's housekeeper, the humourless Mrs Thorne. Emily didn't doubt she would love her child—and she would do so fiercely—but would her child love *her*?

As a daughter she was hardly worth loving; her father had demonstrated that time and again through his rejection of any close bond with her. Who was to say she'd prove any more lovable as a parent?

And then, as if her insecurities weren't enough to unsettle her, there was her mother's death to consider. The frightening reminder of life's utter fragility.

What if childbirth put Emily at a similar risk?

She felt the prick of tears and mentally rolled her eyes. *Great.* Another symptom of pregnancy. She wondered if she could also blame her newly discovered condition for the heavy, achy sensation in her breasts or, like the hot flush, did that have more to do with the man hunkered beside the bed and the desire that flooded her body every time she looked at him?

'I'm tired,' she said, lowering her gaze before her eyes betrayed her. The man had just held her hair as she hurled up the last contents of her stomach. He was unlikely to find her attractive right now. 'Thanks for checking on me.' She curled onto her side and pulled the duvet up to her chin. 'I'm going to try to get some more sleep.'

Ramon stood up and she closed her eyes, listening for the tell-tale sounds of him leaving her room and going back to his. But the absolute silence told her he hadn't moved. Her heart thudded in her ears, and then she felt his hand brush gently over her hair. Felt his lips press a soft, feather-light kiss on her temple. 'We'll do this together, Emily,' he said, his breath fanning warmth across her cheek. 'You're not alone now.' And then he padded out of the room.

As the door closed Emily's chin wobbled dangerously and she tucked her face into the pillow. Yesterday, walking into her empty flat after visiting her doctor, she'd felt very alone but had told herself it didn't matter.

She was used to being alone.

*You're not alone now.*

She drifted off to sleep, that last conscious thought wrapping around her like a warm, comforting cocoon.

# CHAPTER EIGHT

ON THURSDAY EMILY returned to work even though Ramon had wanted her to stay home and rest for the remainder of the week—a preference he'd expressed for the umpteenth time in her kitchen last night. She'd been preparing a simple meal for them and he'd not long been back from a meeting in the city. He'd loosened his tie and collar, rolled his shirt sleeves up his bronzed, muscular forearms and planted his palms on the kitchen island as arguments and counter-arguments had bandied back and forth.

For a brief time Emily had felt as if they were an ordinary couple in the midst of a minor domestic dispute. The thought had left her feeling slightly breathless and flustered, not because it was outlandish or repellent, but rather because it'd sent a flare of unfamiliar warmth through her chest.

No one had ever cared about her enough to argue with her over her choices before.

*He cares about the baby. Not you.*

The insidious thought elbowed its way into her head and she frowned at her computer screen.

Of course he cared about the baby. And that was all that mattered, she assured herself. He was accepting responsibility for the child they'd conceived and Emily wasn't hoping for anything more. Certainly not marriage or any long-term commitment beyond his being a loving, supportive father to their child. If her grandfather had been alive he would have demanded that she wed, but the eccentric, formidable Gordon Royce was no longer here, and not even the outrageous financial incentive laid out in his will could persuade Emily to consider a hasty, loveless marriage. No. She and Ramon would take a sensible, modern-day approach and work out some kind of shared custody arrangement. Ultimately they would lead separate lives while keeping things amicable for the sake of their child.

She clicked her mouse and opened a file on her computer. *Work*. That, if nothing else, would give her a sense of normality, of being in control. And, given that her home and her independence were being seriously encroached upon, she needed to feel in control. Right now she was humouring Ramon, allowing him to assert his dominance because she suspected that underneath all that machismo he, too, was afraid. Who wouldn't be after experiencing the devastating loss of an unborn child? It was why she was willing to tolerate his over-the-top concerns for her safety and wellbeing—for now.

But he couldn't camp in her spare room for the next seven and a half months. It wasn't practical for either of them. He had an office and a home in New York. Clubs and resorts around the world. A jet-setting lifestyle she couldn't imagine him curtailing for long. And she needed her space. Her equilibrium restored. She could barely think straight with all of that potent, simmering testosterone floating about her home.

Which was why she'd been so desperate to return to work. She needed some distance. Some perspective.

A knock sounded on her office door.

'Come in,' she called, glancing up with a twinge of guilt. A closed door sent a message to her staff that she was unavailable. In fact, it was only closed because she'd been making a list of gynaecologists to consider and hadn't got round to re-opening it.

She pasted on a smile that slid off her face the moment the door opened and Ramon stepped in. Exasperated, she glared at him.

He closed the door. 'If I didn't know you were secretly thrilled to see me, *querida*, I'd take offence at that scowl on your face.'

The endearment combined with his dry wit made her heart skip a beat. She sat back in her chair. 'I thought you had meetings all day at Citrine?' She eyed him in his dark pinstriped suit and wondered how many female mouths he'd left watering in his wake that morning. 'Don't you have other places to be besides checking up on me?'

One dark eyebrow lifted. 'Such as?'

'I don't know... New York? Paris? The Arctic Circle?'

He sauntered over and lowered his big frame into a chair in front of her desk. 'You know, you're cute when you're not throwing up.'

She sent him a withering look. 'That's not funny.'

The twitch of his lips suggested he thought otherwise. 'How are you feeling?'

'Fine. As fine as I was feeling an hour ago when you called and asked the same question.'

'Nausea?'

'Better.'

'No more vomiting?'

'Not since this morning.' When yet again he'd knelt on the bathroom floor and held her hair as she'd wretched into the toilet, then carried her back to bed before returning to the spare room. The fact she'd almost grabbed onto him at the last second and implored him to stay in her bed with her was something she'd deliberately avoided dwelling on today. 'Honestly,' she said. 'I'm fine.'

He frowned. '"Fine" is not a term I would apply to someone who is throwing up several times a day.'

'It's just morning sickness. It won't kill me.' She thought of her mother and ruthlessly quashed the inevitable surge of fear.

'Or it could be *hyperemesis gravidarum*.'

She blinked. 'Excuse me?'

'Severe morning sickness,' he said. 'Which could be harmful to both you and the baby.'

She stared at him. 'How do you even *know* that term?'

'It's in one of the booklets on your coffee table. The ones you said your doctor gave to you.' His eyes narrowed. 'You have read them, haven't you?'

She shifted in her chair. 'I'm working my way through them.' It was close to the truth. She'd made a start and then given up when she'd felt overwhelmed by the sheer volume of information. She'd educated herself on the basics—what she should and shouldn't eat, which supplements to take— and that was all she could cope with for now.

'Good.' He stood up. 'Let's go.'

She frowned. 'Where?'

'To lunch.'

She shook her head. 'I'm not hungry.'

'You have to eat, Emily.' His tone grew stern. 'For you and for the baby.'

The knowledge that he was right—she couldn't live entirely on crackers and herbal tea—grated against an instinctive urge to rail against the web of control he was slowly weaving around her. She wasn't accustomed to having her decisions made for her...and yet she understood that he had the best interests of their baby at heart.

And that, she reminded herself once again, was all that mattered right now.

Her baby.

*Their* baby.

She retrieved her handbag from a drawer and stood. 'Very well,' she said, the prospect of trying something other than crackers for lunch not as unappealing as she'd made out. She missed food. Missed her ordinarily healthy appetite.

Before Ramon opened the door, she placed her hand on

his forearm. 'I haven't told anyone yet,' she said. 'Not even Marsha. I'd prefer we keep the pregnancy a secret until I've passed the first trimester.'

'Of course.'

She felt the muscles in his arm tense under her hand and quickly let go. 'You haven't told anyone?'

'No.'

'Not even your family?'

His mouth tightened fractionally. 'No one, Emily.'

Sensing she'd ventured into sensitive territory, she left the subject alone, yet as they exited the club through a discreet side entrance she couldn't help wondering about his family. She'd assumed he would want to tell them almost straight away about the pregnancy but clearly that wasn't the case. For a moment she thought that was strange and then it occurred to her that she was the last person qualified to make that kind of determination.

What did *she* know about family?

Sadly, not a lot.

On Saturday morning Ramon flew to Paris to meet with a team of engineers at Saphir. Apparently there was some structural issue with the enormous swimming pool in the recreation centre and a dispute with the original installation company that was sufficiently serious for him to involve himself.

He'd urged Emily to go with him, but she'd refused. Returning to Paris, to the same place where they'd shared their one night of incredible, mind-blowing sex, would do neither of them any favours. Sharing her home with him, sleeping in separate rooms while every night she yearned for his touch, was challenging enough without stirring up memories safer left buried. Reluctant to leave her alone even for a single night, Ramon had argued, and their heated exchange had acted like lighter fluid on an already blazing fire, ramping up the sexual tension that'd simmered below the surface of their every interaction in the last five days.

Tired and irritable by the week's end, Emily had told herself she was looking forward to his absence.

Now, after twenty-four hours without his overwhelming, charismatic presence in her home, she had to admit the truth.

She missed him.

Which was lunacy. How could you miss someone who'd been a fixture in your life for less than a week?

She frowned into the bowl of brownie batter she was mixing by hand with a solid wooden spoon. Allowing herself to grow dependent on Ramon would be a mistake. Whatever form their relationship eventually took, he would be there for their child, not for her. And that suited Emily just fine. She needed him to step up and be a father—a better one, hopefully, than Maxwell had been to her—but she didn't need him to be anything else. Not in the long term.

Curbing her thoughts, she focused on her baking. This morning, for the first time in a week, her nausea had been short-lived and mild enough to avoid a sprint to the bathroom. Taking advantage of the unexpected reprieve, she'd gone for a walk in the autumn sunshine, picked up some fresh produce from a local market, indulged in an early-afternoon nap and then awoken with a fierce, irrepressible craving for chocolate.

She stopped stirring, dipped her finger into the batter for a taste test and closed her eyes as she let her taste buds reach a verdict. The balance of the dark chocolate and the vanilla was perfect. Sliding her finger out of her mouth, she hummed her approval.

'*Dios.*'

Emily almost screamed with fright at the deep, gruff

voice that echoed through her kitchen. She flattened her palm over her racing heart and turned.

Ramon stood in the doorway, one powerful shoulder propped against the frame, the compact leather holdall he travelled with sitting on the hardwood floor at his feet. In a casual open-necked shirt and thigh-hugging jeans, he looked rugged, gorgeous and a thousand times more mouthwatering than any brownie batter.

A rush of need tightened her belly. 'I thought you weren't getting back till later!'

His gaze slid over her, leaving a trail of heat in its wake. 'Why are you cooking in your underwear?'

Her cheeks burned and she silently cringed. Her pink knickers were the old, practical cotton ones she wore for comfort, and she knew without looking that her stretchy white camisole did little to conceal the fact she was bra-less. She resisted folding her arms over her breasts. 'I went for a nap.'

He straightened. 'Are you unwell?'

She stopped herself from executing an exasperated eye roll. 'No. I was just tired. When I woke up I was craving something sweet and… I was hot…' It was her only excuse for not having thrown her clothes back on after her nap. She cast him an accusing look. 'Why did you creep in?'

One corner of his mouth lifted. 'I didn't "creep". I came in quietly in case you were resting.' He pushed away from the door frame, his gaze trailing over her again, and there was something very deliberate about the way he looked at her. 'So you're feeling okay?'

She swallowed, her mouth gone dry. 'Yes.' Was her imagination running wild or was the gleam in his eyes almost predatory? She cleared her throat. 'Did you get the problem with the pool sorted?'

'*Sí.*'

He moved closer and her skin started to tingle. She pressed her back against the edge of the bench. 'Will you need to return next week?'

'No. Did you miss me, Emily?'

Struggling to keep her breathing even, she shrugged. 'Not really.'

One dark eyebrow rose. 'Not at all?'

He moved another inch closer and her limbs weakened. 'Maybe a tiny bit,' she relented.

He braced his hands on the counter either side of her. 'I missed you.'

His voice was low and gravel-rough, and a pulse of excitement flickered in Emily's throat. She sent her tongue out across her lower lip to alleviate its dryness and heard his breath catch. Raw desire flared in his eyes, and the look of intense arousal on his face, the palpable throb of leashed energy from his big body, was enthralling. Intoxicating. He wanted her, and his patent hunger called on some deep, primitive level to her own equally ravenous desire.

'What are you making?'

She saw his mouth move, saw those sensuous lips form the words, but couldn't comprehend the question. 'What?' she asked faintly.

He tipped her chin up, forcing her gaze to lift from his beautiful mouth. 'What are you making?' he repeated.

This close, she could see the tiny individual pinpricks of the dark stubble along his jaw, feel the impact of the raw heat radiating off him. It shimmered in the air, saturating her skin, slowing the blood in her veins to a sluggish, sensual beat.

She managed to articulate a response. 'Chocolate brownies.'

'Doesn't chocolate contain caffeine?'

As if drawn by the pull of a powerful magnet, her gaze returned to his mouth.

'Are you going to lecture me,' she challenged huskily, 'or kiss me?'

Ramon slid his mouth over Emily's and drank in her sweet taste like a man savouring his first sip of water after days trapped in a merciless desert.

Except his deprivation and thirst had lasted for weeks, not days, and this last week had proven by far the most torturous.

Four nights of sleeping in her spare room. Four nights of doing the right thing. Four nights of struggling to dampen the hot embers of desire that constantly threatened to burst into flame and incinerate his restraint, along with his questionable attempts at chivalry.

And the mornings… The mornings were their own special brand of hell. Each time she was sick, a gut-wrenching combination of powerlessness and disgust tore at him. *Self*-disgust because, even as he carried her back to bed after a bout of illness, his body stirred with an untimely lust he had no ability to switch off.

Last night in Paris had offered no reprieve. And not only because of the constant, gnawing concern about her welfare that he knew in some part of his brain was irrational and extreme. He'd stayed in the same suite they'd shared seven weeks before and realised too late his mistake. Every inch of the place, from the living room, to the bed, to the shower, had teased hot, erotic images from his memory until desire had pounded through him so relentlessly he'd had to rely on his hand to achieve a degree of release.

Flying back today, he'd been as grimly and ruthlessly determined as ever to keep his lust banked and his hands to himself—and then he'd walked in and found her standing in her underwear in the kitchen, with her glorious mane of hair flowing loose over her shoulders and her finger in her mouth like some provocative magazine centrefold.

God forgive him.

He was only human.

Her hands in his hair, her soft body moulded to his, she moaned against his lips, a low, needy sound that ramped up the heat in his body and assured him that she was a willing, enthusiastic participant. Reluctantly, he dragged his mouth from hers. If he didn't press pause he'd end up taking her right there against the kitchen bench, or on the floor. He gathered her into his arms, strode from the kitchen and halted in the hallway.

Intuiting his quandary, she whispered in his ear. 'My room.'

Seconds later he lowered her onto her bed and ripped off her scant attire in between pressing hot, urgent kisses to her mouth and throat. When he had her completely naked, he groaned. Her creamy skin was smooth and flawless, her breasts as perfect as he remembered, perhaps even a little fuller. He drew one of her rosy nipples into his mouth and she arched up, drove her hands into his hair and encouraged him with little mewls of delight that intensified the throb of his desire.

She tugged at his shirt, her fingers fumbling with a button. 'Not fair,' she panted. 'I'm the only one naked.'

To which he gave a low chuckle, reluctantly left her side and quickly dispensed with his clothing. Naked, he returned, straddling her legs so he could admire the view while tracing the curves of her body with his hands.

Her stomach was flat, no sign of the life growing inside her evident as yet. But knowing it was there—knowing they'd created it together—flooded him with a fierce sense of possessiveness far more potent than any fear he'd wrestled with in recent days.

The child inside her was his.

*She was his.*

He leaned over and kissed Emily's stomach, glancing up as she lifted her head. Their gazes locked and it seemed in those few seconds, with only the sounds of their breathing and the drum of his heartbeat filling his ears, as if something unspoken and powerful passed between them. He dragged his gaze from hers before the strange pressure in his chest could intensify, then went lower, down to the sweet, feminine centre of her body. Gently, he parted her and found her wet and swollen. He slipped his finger inside her, loving the way she panted and writhed.

'Come for me, *mi belleza*,' he commanded, then licked once, and she climaxed almost immediately.

'Ramon!'

Gasping his name, she dove her fingers into his hair, gripping his scalp as he sucked and licked, extending her orgasm until her keen cries of pleasure became soft whimpers and her whole body went limp. He rose up between her legs, his body taut with tension, his muscles trembling from the effort required to contain his need. He was afraid that, if he plunged into her now, he'd lose control and take her too hard and fast. *Dios*. Was it possible to hurt the baby?

He rolled onto his back and took her with him so that she sat astride him. Grasping her hips, he positioned her above his erection. This way she'd have control. She seemed to understand because she reached down, wrapped her fingers around his aching shaft and guided the tip to her entrance. For a second he tensed, automatically thinking, *Condom*, then realised they didn't need one. He closed his eyes and couldn't stop a rough cry ripping from his throat as she sank onto him, encasing him in a sheath of silken heat.

Teeth gritted, he kept his pelvis as still as possible, allowing Emily to set the pace and decide how deep to take him. She began to move, her tight, wet heat sliding up and down his shaft, and Ramon's consciousness narrowed until there was nothing but her sitting atop him, her face contorted with pleasure as she wantonly rode him.

Nothing else filled his head.

No concerns.

No fears.

Just their stunning, mind-blowing chemistry and the shattering pinnacle of a climax more powerful than any he'd ever experienced.

'I've made an appointment for us to see a gynaecologist on Tuesday.'

Emily's head rested on Ramon's chest. She blinked drowsily. His deep voice had registered but she had trouble processing his words. Possibly something to do with the post-coital haze shrouding her brain, she thought with a bloom of lazy satisfaction.

A smile pushed its way onto her mouth. She'd always thought the notion of multiple orgasms was a fallacy, just as she'd always believed she would never be someone who enjoyed sex very much.

Now she knew better.

On both counts.

She thought about the brownie batter, abandoned on the kitchen counter, and smiled again. Who needed chocolate when you could have…?

Suddenly her limbs went from languid to rigid. 'What did you say?' She tried to sit up but his arms tightened, keeping her locked against his side. 'Let me go,' she demanded.

'No.'

His abrupt refusal sent a pulse of anger through her. 'Why not?'

'Because you're about to get upset.'

'I'm already upset,' she snapped.

'All the more reason to stay here and calm down.'

Furious, she struggled against him, but he was too strong, his arms like bands of solid steel, his big, muscular thighs trapping one of her own. 'Fine,' she bit out after a moment of angry panting and mental cursing. 'At least let me look at you properly.'

He loosened his hold, just a fraction—enough for her to twist around. The movement brought her breasts into full contact with his chest, and she ignored the puckering of her nipples, the strum of heat in her belly. They were both naked still, the sheets tangled around their feet, the air heavily scented with sex. She looked at him expectantly, and he blew out a breath.

'You were taking too long to decide on a specialist,' he said. 'So I made the decision for us.'

*'Us?'*

'Yes, Emily. Us.' He propped a hand behind his head, his biceps bunching impressively, and stared down the length of his nose at her. The strong, proud quality of that particular appendage reminded her that many generations of Spanish aristocracy ran through his blood. 'It's my baby too.'

His tone chided, and she felt uncomfortably as if she'd been slapped on the wrist. 'But it's my body,' she countered. 'I should get to choose who looks after it.' The fact she hadn't done so yet was beside the point. Damn it, she was pregnant. She was allowed to be indecisive.

'And when were you planning to make your decision?'

'Soon,' she prevaricated.

'Well, now you don't need to. I've done you a favour.'

'No, you haven't. You've swooped in and taken control again as if—' She stopped and drew her bottom lip between her teeth.

'As if I'm the child's father?'

A tense silence descended. She couldn't argue with that simple truth. Then again, she wasn't in a terribly rational mood. She set her jaw. 'I'm not going.'

He scowled. 'You will.'

'I won't.'

'Now you're being childish.'

'What are you going to do?' She gave him an arch look. 'Spank me?'

He growled and moved so fast she was spread-eagled on her stomach before she'd taken her next breath. A large, heavy palm in the centre of her back kept her playfully pinioned to the mattress with her bottom helplessly bared.

She twisted her head to glare at him. 'Don't you dare!'

His grin was wicked and devastatingly sexy. He didn't spank her—she hadn't really thought he would—but he did hold her down, run his hand up the inside of her thigh and do things with his fingers, and later his tongue, that made her whimper, plead and promise to do absolutely anything he commanded.

Afterwards, they lay together again, Emily's cheek pressed to his chest, one arm flung over the hard, beautifully sculpted surface of his abdomen.

'Which gynaecologist?'

He told her the name and her eyes widened. He had chosen a Harley Street specialist. One she had struck from her list of potential private ob-gyns because the cost was too prohibitive and he was bound to have a waiting list.

Clearly, there were certain benefits to be reaped when the father of one's baby was a billionaire.

Her gaze drifted to the pearl necklace lying on the nightstand. Feeling hot and sticky earlier, she'd taken it off before her nap and forgotten to put it back on.

The pearl was the only possession she had of her mother's. Surprisingly, her father had given it to her. He'd left it in a small velvet box on her bedroom dressing table in her grandfather's mansion a few days before her sixteenth birthday, while she'd still been at boarding school. There'd been a handwritten note with it—nothing elaborate, just three short sentences in her father's untidy scrawl:

> *This belonged to your mother.*
> *She would have wanted you to have it.*
> *Happy Birthday.*
> *Maxwell*

Not *Love, Dad*.

Just *Maxwell*.

Her throat tightened. She'd heard people say you couldn't miss something you'd never had, but Emily knew that wasn't true. She'd never known her mother, but she had missed her desperately throughout her life. When Emily was ten, Mrs Thorne, in a rare moment of compassion, had given her two photographs of her mother and she had cherished them, looking at them often and longing to know more about the woman with the wild blonde curls and the pretty smile. But Mrs Thorne, when asked, had said she hadn't known Kathryn very well and had told Emily to ask her father.

It had taken Emily six months to work up the courage to broach the subject during one of his infrequent visits, and then Maxwell had brushed her curiosity aside.

Closing her eyes, she held her breath and listened to the sound of Ramon's heart beating. It was strong and power-ful, much like the man himself. How had she ever drawn parallels between Ramon and her father? They weren't cut from the same cloth. She saw that now.

If her mother had had someone like Ramon by her side during her pregnancy, ensuring she received the proper care and attention, would she have lived?

Emily would never know the answer. She would never know her mother and she could do nothing to change that. But she could do everything within her power to ensure *her* child would grow up knowing its mother.

'I'll go to the appointment on Tuesday,' she said softly, and he kissed the top of her head.

*'Gracias, mi belleza.'*

# CHAPTER NINE

Mr Lindsay, the Harley Street specialist, was a mild-mannered, softly spoken man to whom Emily warmed at once despite the nerves jangling in her belly in the hours leading up to the appointment. As an expectant mother she felt as if she should be more excited about her first prenatal visit, but it simply made a situation she still grappled to cope with all the more stark and real.

Mr Lindsay smiled from the other side of his big desk in his big, plush medical suite. 'Do you have a rough idea of when you conceived?'

Emily felt her face flame. Was it normal to know the exact date you'd conceived? Or did that scream *one-night stand*?

Just as she opened her mouth to stammer out an answer, Ramon smoothly intervened, supplying the date and then adding, 'We think it was around then, at any rate.' From the chair beside hers, he gave her a warm, encouraging smile. 'It's hard to say exactly, isn't it, *querida*?'

She nodded, returned his smile and tried to transmit a 'thank you' with her eyes.

She was glad he was there—a turnaround from this morning, admittedly, when she'd told him she'd prefer to come alone. A waste of breath, of course. He'd been adamant about attending with her, and no argument had come close to changing his mind.

Mr Lindsay did a swift calculation and pronounced a due date, and Emily's breath locked in her lungs for a moment. In just under thirty-one weeks her baby would be born. Suddenly, it all felt very real.

And very frightening.

She tried to focus, answering Mr Lindsay's questions to the best of her ability. After a while her head spun. The checklist was exhaustive. Medications, supplements, health conditions…

'Any family history of miscarriages or complications with pregnancy?'

Emily froze. She'd anticipated the question, but now the time was here the words jammed in her throat. A chill rippled over her skin—a whisper of the fear she'd tried until now to ignore—and she shivered. The seconds stretched and her silence grew awkward, embarrassing, but still she couldn't unlock her voice. And then Ramon reached over and closed his fingers around hers, stilling their shaking. He squeezed, his touch firm. Reassuring. She looked down at their joined hands, the panic abating, then inhaled deeply. 'My mother died in childbirth,' she said.

Mr Lindsay looked up from his notes. 'Your birth?'

'Yes.'

His expression was grave. 'I'm very sorry,' he said. 'Do you know the details?'

'Not really. I think it might have been pre-eclampsia.'

He scribbled a note, then put his pen down and clasped his hands together on his desk. He stared directly into her eyes. 'Emily, it's perfectly natural given your history to feel some fear about your pregnancy,' he said, 'but I want to assure you both—' he glanced at Ramon, then back at Emily '—that you'll be receiving exceptional care throughout every stage of your journey. We'll take extra precautions, with frequent check-ups and regular testing, and keep a close watch on your blood pressure.' He smiled reassuringly. 'We'll do a physical exam and an ultrasound today to check everything is fine,' he continued. 'There won't be much to see, however. It will be another six weeks at least until we can determine your baby's sex.'

'Oh.' She blinked. Did she want to know her baby's sex

before it was born? She glanced uncertainly at Ramon. Would it matter to him if their child was a girl or a boy? It didn't matter to Emily. And the crazy clause in her grandfather's will certainly didn't sway her one way or another. Gordon Royce had been a fool to attach such an outrageous condition to a large part of his legacy. Even if she had a boy she wouldn't accept the money. It could go to charity for all she cared. 'I don't think I want to know that anyway,' she said. 'I mean—' she glanced again at Ramon '—I'd rather it was a surprise, if you don't mind.'

He shrugged. 'Of course.'

Half an hour later, her first prenatal check-up was over. Ramon had sat in the waiting room while she'd undergone the exam and the ultrasound. She emerged and smiled at him. His coming with her today had shifted something and their connection felt less tenuous, less fragile. It was something Emily hadn't experienced before—a close connection with another person. It gave her hope. Hope that her bond with her baby would be strong. That she'd be a good mother. *That her child would love her.*

Ramon held her hand as they stepped out into the warm autumn sunshine. Outside, they paused on the pristine Mayfair pavement, waiting for his driver to arrive. Emily looked up at him, at those gorgeous, perfectly landscaped features, and her heart performed a slow somersault in her chest. She opened her mouth, wanting to thank him, to tell him how much his support meant to her today, but a bright pop of light stopped her in her tracks.

'Mr de la Vega! Who's the lady? Is she knocked up? Is it yours?'

The lone paparazzo fired off another round of shutter clicks. Scowling, Ramon turned Emily into him, cupping the back of her head and pressing her face protectively into his shoulder.

'When's the kid due?'

Ramon swore under his breath, and then their car pulled up and he was bundling her into the back of the sleek black sedan. The second they were safely ensconced, the driver sped off. Heart pounding, Emily sucked in a shaky breath and cast a stricken look at Ramon.

His face was thunderous.

'You'll marry her, I assume.'

The statement carried a faint air of command. Ramon gritted his teeth. If he could have reached down the phone line and strangled his brother with his bare hands, he would have. There were never any grey areas with Xavier. Life was comprised of black and white.

Right and wrong.

Do or don't.

Right now Xav was urging him towards the 'do'. More specifically, the words 'I do'.

'I'll make that decision when I'm ready.'

A short silence. 'You *are* taking responsibility for the child?'

Ramon ground his teeth a little harder. Xav's opinion of him really did scrape the bottom of the barrel. 'Of course,' he bit out.

He curled his hand into a fist on the desk top and absently cast his gaze over the office that had belonged to Maxwell Royce. In recent days Ramon had staked a more permanent claim on the space, using it as his main base from which to work while in London. He leaned back in the chair, his mind working overtime as it had for the past twenty-four hours. Perhaps he should stake a more permanent claim on the man's daughter as well. It wasn't as if he hadn't already entertained the idea many times over.

'Mamá and Papá are upset they had to find out this way.'

Ramon couldn't help but hear the implicit criticism in his brother's voice. The unspoken words.

*You've hurt them. Again.*

'Why did you not tell us?' Xav demanded.

'We haven't told anyone. It's too soon. The pregnancy was only confirmed last week.'

'Did you not think the photos would surface?'

He'd thought, *hoped*, they would make a small, scarcely visible splash. Certainly here in England that had been the case, thanks to a minor royal and her very public skirmish with law enforcement dominating the tabloids. Spain was a different story, however. Every gossip site had picked up the photograph of him and Emily standing outside a Harley Street gynaecologist's clinic. In addition, the shot taken of them outside Saphir in Paris over seven weeks ago had surfaced.

'The photos are unfortunate,' he said tightly.

A heavy sigh came down the line. 'Hector's been on the phone. He's on his high horse again. He says the board will have some natural concerns about the potential for negative reaction from our more conservative shareholders.'

'Tell Hector he can go scr—'

'I did.'

Ramon leaned back in his chair. His cool, diplomatic brother had told Hector where to go? That was a conversation he would have liked to witness.

'But he has a point.' Xav's voice was weary. 'This kind of publicity could have a negative impact on both the business and the family.' He was silent. 'Marry the Royce woman and make this right, Ramon. It's what Mamá and Papá will expect. Make them happy. Don't bring disgrace on the family.'

He didn't add the word 'again', but he didn't need to.

The inference was loud and clear.

* * *

'I made you some tea.' Marsha walked across the office and placed a mug of steaming liquid on Emily's desk. 'It's ginger,' she said. 'For the nausea.'

Emily managed a grateful smile. 'Thanks.'

'Can I do anything else?'

'No. Thank you. You're doing plenty. Have there been many more calls?'

A scowl formed on Marsha's pretty face. 'Those tabloid journalists are scum,' she declared. 'Honestly, the things they have the nerve to ask—' She broke off, perhaps seeing Emily's silent wince. Quickly, she added, 'But they're not worth fretting over. And they're not getting anything from me but a "no comment".'

Emily nodded, gratitude surging again. From the moment her pregnancy had become fodder for the tabloids, her assistant had been a godsend. Seventy-two hours of online speculation and gossip had taken its toll, however, and it seemed even Marsha's sweet, patient disposition was being tested.

Emily waited until the younger woman had left before dropping her head in her hands. Humiliation swamped her. This was not how she'd wanted her pregnancy revealed to the world. It was embarrassing and intrusive, and she didn't want even to think about the impact it could have on The Royce. So often she'd swept her father's scandalous behaviour under the carpet, condemning him for his irresponsibility and lack of discretion. Not once had she ever imagined that *she* would cause a scandal.

At least they hadn't made the front page of the papers, although the online gossip sites were having a field day. Emily had fought her curiosity until a moment of weakness had struck. She'd regretted the impulse as soon as she'd clicked on the photo of her and Ramon standing outside the clinic. It made her want to crawl into a very deep hole and never come out. The paparazzo had snapped them just as she had looked up at Ramon, and the expression on her face…

*Oh, God.*

A fresh wave of humiliation struck. The photo made her look besotted. Infatuated. *In love.* Which was ridiculous. Yes, they were sleeping together—something she knew they'd have to stop doing eventually—but she wasn't in love with him. How could she be? She didn't know the first thing about love.

'Emily.'

She jerked her head up, an immediate shiver running down her spine. She mightn't love Ramon, but his deep voice nevertheless held the power to elicit a swift, visceral response. He moved from the doorway, a mouthwatering mix of raw masculinity and sharp, sophisticated style. He didn't own a single suit that didn't fit his broad frame to utter perfection. The casual look he sported in the evenings in her home was the one she'd come to prefer of late, however. Faded jeans, tee shirt and bare feet. Until recently, she hadn't realised how sexy a man's feet could be.

'Emily?'

She started. 'Sorry?'

'I asked if you're all right.'

'Of course.' A lie. She was a mass of tension and nerves.

'Do you have much more work to do?'

Bereft of her usual focus and energy, she looked at the report on her desk. The one she'd stared blankly at for the last hour. She glanced at her watch. It was only four o'clock. 'A bit,' she said.

'Finish up and come with me.'

She frowned at his commanding tone. 'Where?'

'It's a surprise.'

'You know I don't like surprises.'

His smile was gentle enough to melt her insides. And her resistance.

'Humour me,' he said.

An hour later Emily stood in the centre of an enormous living room on the lower floor of a beautiful late nineteenth-century mansion in Chelsea.

'What do you think?'

Slowly, she turned and looked at Ramon. He stood in front of the big window that overlooked the large fenced-in front garden, rays of late-afternoon sunshine highlighting the rich, glossy mahogany of his hair. His jacket was undone, his tie was loosened and his hands were thrust casually into his trouser pockets.

Emily wasn't fooled, however.

Every hard inch of him radiated tension.

She gazed up at the moulded ceiling and the beautiful, intricate glass chandelier above her head. 'It's stunning.' More than stunning, she thought. Even unfurnished, the three-storey, seven-bedroom residence was breathtaking.

Having grown up in her grandfather's mansion north of London, she wasn't unaccustomed to large houses. But, while the interior of her grandfather's home had been characterised by dark wood and heavy, oppressive furnishings, this house was light and airy, its preserved period features interspersed with touches of contemporary luxury that gave it an elegant, timeless appeal.

And the kitchen!

Emily had salivated over the walk-in pantry, the giant stove, the hand-crafted cabinetry with oodles of storage space and the massive custom-designed granite countertops offering plenty of room for culinary experimentation.

Her heart had soared with excitement, and then just as quickly had dropped.

This was a 'for ever' home. The kind where kids grew up

and couples grew old. Where families laughed and argued
and loved and cried. Where children and grandchildren
came back for Christmases and birthdays and boisterous
reunions—the kind you saw in movies or read about in
books that guaranteed you a happy ending.

It wasn't the sort of home a billionaire playboy considered buying.

Sadness weighted her down. 'Ramon,' she whispered, a
wealth of feeling and helplessness pouring into that single
utterance of his name.

His gaze held hers and she thought maybe he understood. Thought he might be experiencing some of the same
turmoil she was. He crossed to where she stood and curled
his hands over her shoulders. She wanted to press a finger
against his lips so he couldn't say the words, but her limbs
were frozen, her breath locked in her chest.

'Marry me.'

She closed her eyes. 'I can't.'

He was silent a moment. 'You're saying that because
you're scared.'

She lifted her lids. 'Aren't you?'

A muscle worked in his jaw. 'Yes,' he confessed, the
word seeming to drag from the depths of his throat. 'But
fear isn't a reason to avoid doing the right thing.'

She drew a deep breath. 'Is that what we'd be doing?
The right thing?'

His brows lowered. 'Of course.'

'How do you know it's the right thing?' she challenged
softly.

His eyes hardened a fraction. 'Providing our child with
a stable home with both parents isn't the right thing?'

She swallowed. He painted a nice picture. And, if she let
herself, she could easily indulge the fantasy. Imagine them
living here as husband and wife, raising their child in this

beautiful home. 'Is this what you want, Ramon? A life of domesticity? Tied down with a wife and child?'

His jaw flexed. He dropped his hands from her shoulders. 'I'm thirty years old. Most men settle down eventually.'

Her chest grew heavier. 'I'm not asking what other men do. I'm asking if it's what *you* want. If Paris hadn't happened,' she pressed. 'If I wasn't pregnant, would you be thinking about giving up your bachelor lifestyle?'

'But you are pregnant, Emily.' His voice turned a shade cooler. 'With *my* child.' He paced away, turned back. 'Would you relegate me to the role of part-time father? Someone who breezes in and out of our child's life whenever the custody arrangement tells me I can?'

Emily felt her face blanch. That was exactly the kind of arrangement she'd assumed they would agree upon. But Ramon's description made her blood run cold. Made her think of all the times she'd curled up on her bed as a little girl and cried, believing her daddy didn't care enough to visit her.

A fluttery, panicky feeling worked its way up her throat. 'But what about us?'

He moved closer, eyes narrowing. 'What do you mean?'

'I mean…' she hesitated, colour seeping back into her face '…*us*—our relationship. You're talking about a long-term commitment. Or at least until our child has grown and left home. That could be twenty years, Ramon. Twenty years of commitment to our child…and me. Twenty years with no other…' She hesitated, her chest suddenly constricting.

'Women?' he supplied.

She lifted her chin. 'I won't tolerate that kind of relationship.'

'Marriage,' he corrected. 'We're talking about marriage, Emily. And, yes, I understand the full implications of such a commitment. For the record—' he grasped her chin and locked his gaze on hers '—I won't tolerate that kind of marriage either.'

She blinked. A part of her wanted to believe him. Another part of her said it didn't matter if she believed him or not, because all of this was hypothetical.

Besides, pledging his faithfulness now, when they were still burning up the sheets, was easy. How would his vows hold up when she was heavy and listless with his child, or exhausted from juggling the demands of motherhood and a job?

He clasped her shoulders again. 'We're good together, *querida*. Are you denying that?'

'Lust is hardly a foundation for marriage.'

The hard line of his mouth softened. 'But it's a good starting point, *si*?'

Love was supposed to be the starting point for marriage, she thought. But then what did she know?

She stepped back, forcing his hands to drop. 'It's a beautiful house,' she said, casting a final look around the room. 'But I... I just need some time to think.'

Emily didn't stop thinking. Not for a single waking minute. For the next forty-eight hours, her mind spun and her stomach churned and Ramon waited on her answer with barely leashed impatience.

At two a.m. on Sunday morning she sat on the cushioned window seat in her lounge, staring out at the moonlit night, her mother's pearl tucked in her hand. She laid her other hand over her stomach and knew instinctively the bond she had feared mightn't grow between her and her child was already there. She could feel it with each beat of her heart. A strong, deep connection unlike anything else she'd ever known. It filled her with a fierce resolve to nurture and protect. To do whatever was best for her child. To give it the best life possible and shield him or her from the same bitter hurts and disappointments she'd suffered as a child.

Breathing deeply, she rose and went back to bed. Ramon lay on his back, the white cotton sheet bunched around his waist, his bare chest rising and falling. The sound of his deep, steady breathing was familiar and somehow comforting. She slipped off her robe and climbed between the sheets.

Ramon stirred, his arm lifting so she could curl into his side. 'Emily?' His voice was a sexy, sleep-roughened rumble.

'I'm fine.' She snuggled close and leaned on her elbow. 'Ramon?'

He caressed her hip. *'Si?'*

'Yes,' she said softly.

He went still. And then he deftly turned her onto her back. He didn't say anything. He just stroked his fingers over her hair. Her cheek. Her mouth. And then he kissed her. Long, deep and hard.

# CHAPTER TEN

'Are you close with your brother?'

Ramon glanced up from his laptop. Emily sat in the seat opposite him in his private jet. In a pale blue trouser suit, with her hair caught loosely in a band over one shoulder, she looked beautiful and flawless in spite of the vomiting spell that had struck shortly before their departure for the airport. Ramon had regarded the sudden resurgence of her nausea as sufficient excuse to cancel their trip to Barcelona, but she had refused to let him postpone the weekend.

Five days had passed since she'd agreed to marry him, three days since he'd placed the enormous radiant-cut diamond on her finger. Two days ago he'd notified his family and afterwards released an announcement to the press. Yesterday, he'd closed the deal on the house in Chelsea.

With each step he'd waited for a sense of panic to set in. Instead, he felt a deep, unmitigated satisfaction. A growing certainty that he was doing the right thing.

He answered Emily's question. 'Not especially.'

'Oh.' She sounded surprised. 'Xavier's adopted, right?'

'Yes. But that's not a factor in our relationship. We have different personalities, that's all. Sometimes we clash.' He closed his laptop, noting Emily's hands fidgeting in her lap. 'You're nervous,' he observed.

'A bit. I'm afraid the whole family thing is rather alien to me.'

*Little wonder*, he thought. She'd grown up with an absentee father and no mother. By her own account, the closest thing she'd had to a maternal influence as a child had been her grandfather's housekeeper, who she described as an austere woman whose one saving grace had been teaching Emily to bake and cook.

'Have you heard from your father?'

She shook her head, her mouth turning down, and Ramon knew a fierce desire to find Maxwell Royce and hurt him. The man's daughter was pregnant and engaged and he hadn't bothered to return her calls. Out of courtesy, Ramon had left a message on his phone the day before the engagement was made official, but Royce hadn't responded.

'Why The Royce?' he asked, voicing a question that had been lodged in his brain like an annoying burr for weeks.

'What do you mean?'

'You're smart, dedicated, hard-working. You could have done anything,' he said. 'Chosen any number of professions. Why carve out your career there?'

Colour swept her cheeks. 'When I inherited half of the club, I had no choice but to step up.'

'But you devoted yourself to The Royce long before then.'

She frowned. 'It's my family's business.' A defensive edge crept into her voice. 'Why wouldn't I get involved?' Her expression became shuttered. Averting her face, she looked out of the window at a bank of solid cloud, effectively ending the conversation. But, slowly, her gaze came back to his. 'Actually, there's more to it than that...' She hesitated, her throat moving around a tight swallow. 'I think, in the beginning, I was looking for some kind of connection.'

'To your father?'

'Yes. And to my grandfather. I wasn't close to either one of them, but they were the only family I had. Working at The Royce gave us some common ground. I suppose I wanted to prove myself. To earn their respect. Their attention.'

Ramon felt a tugging deep in his chest. No young person

should have to earn attention from a parent. His dislike of Maxwell Royce strengthened.

'What about you?' she asked, swiftly diverting the focus from herself. 'You gave up an architectural career to join your family's business. Do you miss being an architect?'

'Yes and no,' he hedged. 'I often have a hand in the design and renovation of the clubs and properties under my purview, so I still get to dabble.'

'It must be amazing to have a creative talent.' Her voice was wistful.

'You don't see yourself as creative?'

'Not really.' She wrinkled her perfect nose. 'The most creative I get is baking.'

'I like it when you bake.'

She gave him a pert look. 'Correction. You like it when I bake in my underwear.'

He couldn't hold back a grin. On impulse, he reached for her left hand and pressed a kiss on her knuckles—just above the glittering diamond that proudly proclaimed to the world she was his. A smile softened her face and his mood lightened. Perhaps, with Emily by his side, he wouldn't find this weekend with his family too painful.

Emily sensed a dark storm of tension building within Ramon from the second the jet's wheels touched down in Barcelona. During the flight he'd been happy to talk and their conversation had distracted her from her nerves. Now, as they travelled in the back of a chauffeur-driven SUV to his parents' villa, he was silent and brooding.

Did he not get along with his family? The thought sent a shaft of dismay through her. If his relationship with them was strained, how would they receive *her*? Would they welcome her as a daughter-in-law? Or would she be the scarlet woman who'd trapped their son into marriage by getting herself pregnant?

She looked at the enormous rectangular diamond that glittered on her ring finger. Set in platinum and flanked by two sapphires and clusters of smaller diamonds on either side, it was a beautiful piece of artistry which had drawn a shocked gasp from her when he'd slipped it onto her finger. But after three days it still felt heavy and unfamiliar on her hand—as alien and disconcerting as the experience of meeting his family was going to be.

Her stomach threatening to rebel again, she rummaged in her handbag for a piece of crystallised ginger and popped it in her mouth.

Twenty minutes and three pieces of ginger later, their driver turned off the road and drove between two massive gated pillars. A long tree-lined driveway dappled with early-evening sunlight eventually opened onto lush, colourful gardens and led to a circular courtyard at the front of a magnificent two-storey villa. Before the vehicle had stopped, the villa's big front door swung open and a slender, casually dressed woman emerged.

She was beautiful. A generation older than Emily, but still trim and fit-looking in white trousers and a simple sleeveless burnt orange top. Dark chin-length hair streaked with the odd strand of grey was tucked behind her ears, revealing a stunning bone structure that bore such a striking resemblance to Ramon's, Emily knew at once that this was Elena de la Vega, his mother.

She smiled broadly as they exited the vehicle, then stepped towards her son, her arms extended. She spoke to him in Spanish and Emily didn't understand the words, but she heard affection in the older woman's voice, and saw the shimmer of restrained tears in her eyes. Her emotion, so visible and patently heartfelt, made Emily's chest squeeze. But when mother and son embraced, Ramon was stiff, the hug he gave his mother awkward-looking in spite of Elena's obvious delight at seeing her son.

Emily had no time to dwell on the odd dynamic. Elena turned, clasped Emily's hands in both of hers and squeezed. 'And you are Emily,' she declared, her English accented but perfect. Her eyes shone, a rich shade of caramel-brown like her son's. 'It is a great pleasure to meet you.'

'And you, Mrs de la Vega.'

'Elena,' she insisted. 'My goodness, you are beautiful.' She touched Emily's cheek, her eyes glistening again. 'Come.' She motioned them towards the villa. 'Vittorio has been feeling breathless today so he's resting in the salon before dinner. But he is looking forward to seeing you both.'

As they headed indoors, Ramon placed his palm in the small of Emily's back and murmured in her ear. 'My mother can get a little over-emotional.'

'It's fine,' she whispered, wondering why he felt the need to apologise. Elena de la Vega was delightful.

Vittorio de la Vega turned out to be a tall, commanding man who looked reasonably well, despite the heart problems Ramon had briefly mentioned on the plane. He greeted his son with a firm handshake, then welcomed his future daughter-in-law with an infusion of warmth similar to his wife's, if less effusive. After kissing Emily on both cheeks, he politely enquired about their journey, then offered her a choice of non-alcoholic beverages. The subtle deference to her pregnancy made her blush, but she saw no outward sign of judgement or disapproval.

'Have you set a wedding date?'

Elena posed the question the moment they were all settled on comfortable sofas in the beautiful, high-ceilinged salon.

'Elena,' Vittorio gently chided. He sent Emily an apologetic look. 'You must forgive my wife. She can be very excitable.'

Elena flicked an elegant hand, unperturbed. 'I've recently discovered I'm getting a daughter-in-law *and* a

grandchild. I think a little excitement is perfectly acceptable.' Her warm smile encompassed both Emily and her
son. 'You'll want to get married before the baby arrives,
yes?'

'When we decide on a date, you'll be the first to know,
Mamá,' Ramon said.

If Elena found her son's tone a little too sharp, she gave
no indication. She addressed Emily. 'Your mother must
be very excited.'

Emily stiffened, her gaze shifting to Ramon. Had he told
his family nothing about her? He covered her hand with
his and rubbed his thumb over her knuckles, his eyes offering a form of apology. To Elena, she said, 'My mother
died when I was born. I never knew her.'

'Oh, my dear.' Dismay clouded the older woman's eyes.
'I'm so sorry.' She was silent, as though taking a moment
to respect the depth of Emily's loss. Then, 'I would not
wish to intrude but, if you need help with planning for the
wedding or the baby, I would love nothing more. You may
already know that Ramon and Xavier don't have a sister,
so I've missed out on all the exciting girl things. I would
have loved a daughter...' Her gaze flicked to her son. 'But
when Ramon came along, he was our miracle. We couldn't
have expected another.'

Ramon didn't say anything, but the slight tightening of
his hand over hers betrayed the sudden flare of tension in
his body. She glanced at him again, but his face was im-
passive. Unreadable. Hiding her confusion, she smiled at
Elena. 'Thank you. I'd appreciate that. I think I'm going to
need all the help I can get.' And then, because Ramon's ill
humour was starting to unsettle her, she remarked on the
splendour of the villa and asked Elena for a tour.

Less than an hour later, they sat down to dinner at one
end of a long table in a sumptuous formal dining room.

'Xavier couldn't join us tonight,' Elena said, her tone apologetic. 'But he'll be here tomorrow.'

Vittorio poured wine for the table and a sparkling grape juice for Emily. 'Have you been to Barcelona before?'

'No. This is my first time in Spain.'

Elena clapped her hands together. 'Oh! That's very exciting. You have so much to see! Ramon, where will you take her first?'

For the first time since they'd walked off the plane, a relaxed smile curved his mouth. 'Barri Gòtic,' he said.

'Ah. Marvellous,' Elena enthused. 'The old city is magnificent.'

From then on the conversation remained light and flowed throughout the meal. With her nausea gone and the tension dissipated, Emily was able to enjoy the fabulous food served over three courses to the table by a trio of discreet, efficient waiting staff. As the evening grew late, however, she found herself stifling a series of yawns.

'I believe my fiancée needs to retire.'

Ramon's statement elicited a small start of surprise from Emily. Was he really so attuned to the subtleties of her body language? And there she'd been, thinking her efforts to hide her tiredness had been rather stellar.

'Of course.' Elena cast her a sympathetic look. 'You must go and rest. We will have plenty of time over the weekend to talk.'

Upstairs, the suite she and Ramon had been allocated was enormous and just as resplendent as the rest of the villa. Emily dropped onto the end of the majestic four-poster bed, sighed and kicked off her low-heeled sandals. 'Your parents are lovely, Ramon.'

He stripped off his shirt and she admired the impressive expanse of hard muscle and smooth skin. She didn't think she'd ever tire of gazing at his magnificent body. He was truly breathtaking. He toed off his shoes and unbuckled his belt. 'They're good people.'

Emily dragged her gaze away from his taut, flat stomach and that tantalising downward arrow of dark hair. 'But...?' she said softly.

He paused. 'But what?'

She hesitated. 'Did I just imagine the tension earlier?'

He shrugged. 'No family is perfect, Emily.'

Brows tugging together, she opened her mouth to ask why he was being cryptic, but he turned away, shed the rest of his clothing and then straightened to face her.

Emily's mouth dried.

Not only was he standing naked before her...he was erect. Proudly, gloriously erect. Liquid heat pooled between her legs.

Struggling to remember the gist of their conversation, she forced her gaze up. 'Is this your best attempt to avoid talking?'

One corner of his sinful mouth curled. He tipped her chin up. 'Sleep or sex, Emily?'

If she said sleep, he would leave her alone. Respect her need for rest. But suddenly rest seemed very overrated. And her nausea hadn't recurred in several hours. What was the expression? Make hay while the sun shines? She arched an eyebrow. 'Conversation isn't an option?'

'No.'

'Well, in that case...'

She reached out, curled her fingers around his hot, rigid length and took him into her mouth.

Showing Emily the sights of Barcelona proved a more pleasurable experience than Ramon had anticipated.

Rising early on Saturday, he borrowed one of his father's cars and took her on a scenic coastal drive before heading into the centre of the city. They parked up and

strolled along grand boulevards and winding cobblestone
streets, and he realised it'd been many years since he'd allowed himself to enjoy the energy and vibrancy of the city
he'd loved as a boy. Whenever he returned for business he
kept his visits as short as possible. Now, as he pointed out
iconic landmarks and showed her some of the city's greatest architectural gems, he realised his designer's eye had
missed the unrivalled beauty of Barcelona with its mix of
contemporary, Gothic and mediaeval design.

Barri Gòtic, the Gothic quarter, was still a tangle of old,
narrow stone alleyways and unique, interesting storefronts.
Emily loved it and insisted they explore. When their stom-
achs growled for sustenance, he chose a traditional tapas
bar with art nouveau murals on the walls, lively jazz music
and a reputation for outstanding food.

Whether from pregnancy or the excitement of discover-
ing a new city, Emily glowed. She was beautiful—and she
had charmed his parents, as he hadn't doubted she would.
His mother already adored her. More than that, her presence
had been a balm of sorts, gradually easing the tension in
him. The burning shame and brutal guilt he relived every
time he saw his parents and which, even after twelve years,
made looking his mother in the eye almost impossible.

He reached across the table and tucked a curl behind her
ear as she bit into another savoury croquette. So far today,
no nausea. In fact, her appetite was exceptionally healthy,
not unlike her appetite in bed last night…

'Ramon?'

Jerked from the memory of her lush mouth on him, he
smiled at her, but her attention was elsewhere.

She frowned, looking over his shoulder. 'There's a young
man over there staring at you.'

Twisting round, he followed the line of her gaze.

And felt his stomach muscles clench into a sudden, violent spasm.

*Jorge.*

His spine turned to ice. He blinked, trying to shake the crazy notion from his head. It couldn't be Jorge. Jorge was dead. Ramon knew this. He had watched him die twelve years ago.

The lookalike stood up, started stalking towards their table and a swift bolt of recognition cleared the confusion from Ramon's head.

Slowly, he rose. 'Mateo.'

Mateo Mendoza glared at him with fierce, undiluted hatred blazing in his black eyes. He spoke in Spanish, his voice a low, belligerent snarl. 'You've got a nerve showing your face around here, de la Vega.'

Keeping his cool in the face of the younger man's hostility, Ramon tried to remember how old Jorge's brother had been when he'd last seen him. Twelve? Which would make him twenty-four now.

Another man, roughly the same age, appeared at Mateo's back. He put his hand on his friend's shoulder and murmured something, but Mateo shook him off.

Ramon threw a glance at Emily. A look of startled alarm had settled on her face.

*Dios.*

He didn't want her to witness this. Didn't want her in the middle of a situation he might not be able to control. Body tensed, alert, he focused his attention on Mateo. 'Whatever you want to get off your chest, Mateo,' he growled, 'this is not the place.'

The younger man drew his right arm back and Ramon knew he was about to put his weight behind a punch. He could have ducked, blocked the blow; he was bigger and stronger, so he could take the other man easily. Instead, he braced his shoulders and took the full impact of Mateo's fist on the left side of his jaw. It hurt like hell, making a cracking sound like a gunshot inside his skull.

Emily shot to her feet. 'Ramon!'

'Sit down, Emily,' he gritted out. He didn't want Mateo's attention on her.

'I will not sit down!' she cried. 'What on earth is going on?'

Eyes narrowed, chest heaving, Mateo trawled his gaze over her, a sneer twisting his lips.

Ramon fisted his hands. 'Did that make you feel better, Mateo?' he asked drawing the other man's attention.

Slicing another look at Emily, Mateo jabbed a finger in Ramon's direction. 'This man is a murderer,' he spat in English, and then his friend grabbed his arm and roughly dragged him out of the bar before the burly staff member who was weaving through the tables reached them.

His heart racing, Ramon apologised for the disturbance, paid the bill and added an extra-large gratuity, then took Emily by the elbow and walked her into the street.

In a high-pitched voice, she demanded, 'What on earth was that about?'

Retaining a firm hold on her arm, he headed in the direction of the car. 'Keep walking, Emily.'

'Why did you let him punch you?'

'Because he was angry and needed to vent.'

'By *hitting* you?'

'I deserved it.'

'What do you mean?'

He realised she was panting and slowed his stride a little. 'I'll explain later.'

'He said you were a murderer.'

Ramon clenched his teeth and winced as renewed pain shot through his jaw. 'I heard what he said.'

'Are you going to tell me what he meant?'

'Later,' he repeated.

She fell silent but he sensed her gaze darting back to him, again and again, questioning. Confused. In the car, a thick, heavy silence enveloped them, Emily's rigid posture telegraphing her anger.

He cursed under his breath.

Coming to Barcelona had been a mistake.

When they reached the villa, he stopped the car outside the front steps and kept the engine idling. 'Go inside, Emily.' He felt the weight of her gaze on him, but he looked straight ahead, his hands clenched on the steering wheel.

'Where are you going?'

He didn't know. But he needed some space. He couldn't deal with her questions right now. 'Go inside,' he said hoarsely. 'Please.'

She got out and slammed the door, and he gunned the engine and drove off.

Dinner that evening was a tense, awkward affair, the empty chair beside Emily a painful reminder of the awful incident at the tapas bar.

She still had no clue what the confrontation had been about, but she knew one thing with utter, unequivocal certainty.

Her baby's father was *not* a murderer.

She wished he would come back and tell her that himself. But she hadn't seen him since he'd sped off in a cloud of gravel and dust and brooding testosterone.

Anxiety gnawed at her, diminishing her appetite for the lovely meal in front of her. Question after question tumbled through her head. Where was he? Was he okay? Why hadn't he called? Had he been involved in an accident? Why hadn't he returned for dinner?

*Had he abandoned her?*

Reading her anxiety, Elena said gently, 'He'll be back.'

The man seated across from her gave a derisive snort. 'This is typical of him to run off.'

Xavier's voice vibrated with anger and Emily gripped

her knife and fork, everything within her rebelling against the notion that Ramon had 'run off'.

He wouldn't desert her. Not here. Like this. He could have run at any time in the last three weeks, starting from the moment she'd told him she was pregnant. He hadn't. And she refused to believe he'd done so now.

'I am sorry you had to witness what you did this afternoon.' Xavier spoke to her. 'My brother—'

'Xavier.' Vittorio interrupted his son. 'Emily deserves an explanation, but I think it must come from Ramon.'

Xavier's expression tightened, his intense, somewhat superior gaze flicking back to Emily.

Like his younger brother, he was devastatingly handsome, but far more formidable. Although they weren't genetically related, nature had graced them both with strong, broad-shouldered physiques and stunning facial structures. The most striking contrast Emily could see was their eyes. Where Ramon's were expressive and warm, Xavier's were a cold, hard grey. Not unlike her own, she supposed, though hers were several shades paler and a lot less piercing.

She suppressed a shiver.

Had she been wise to tell them what had happened? When she'd gone inside, bewildered and upset, Xavier had been there with his parents and Elena had seen her stricken expression and immediately put a comforting arm around her. Before Emily had thought better of it, she'd spilled the details of the entire incident.

Distracted, she toyed with the food on her plate.

And then the sound of a car engine and gravel crunching outside had everyone surging to their feet.

Xavier threw down his napkin and stormed out first, a fierce scowl on his face.

Vittorio strode after him.

Emily made to follow, but Elena placed a restraining hand on her arm. 'Give them a few minutes,' she advised.

'My boys have tempers. There might be some fireworks.'
She looped her arm through Emily's. 'Walk with me on
the terrace.'

Emily didn't want to walk. She wanted to go to Ramon.
She wanted to check with her own eyes that he was all right.
*She wanted the explanation she was owed.*

No sooner had they stepped onto the terrace than the
arguing commenced outside the front of the villa. Raised
male voices carried clearly on the still evening air and she
heard Xavier, then Ramon, and his deep, familiar bari-
tone made her heart clench in her chest. Vittorio wasn't as
loud—the mediator between his sons, she assumed. They
spoke in rapid-fire Spanish, frustrating her attempts to understand. And then their voices grew muffled, suggesting
they'd moved into the house and closeted themselves in a
room.

Emily's breath shuddered out, a deep sigh of despair. 'I
don't understand any of this.'

Elena hugged Emily's arm as they strolled. 'I'm afraid
things have been strained in our family for a long time.
Ramon has struggled to move on from the past—from the
mistakes he made as a boy—and he believes that, because
he hasn't done so, we haven't either.'

Emily looked at her. 'But you have?'

'Of course. I love my son. I always have. I never stopped
loving him—he simply stopped allowing himself to *be*
loved.'

Why? Because he believed he didn't deserve love? A
deep ache spread through Emily's chest.

Elena sat down on a cushioned rattan sofa and urged
Emily to sit beside her. 'Everything will be fine. You'll see.'

Emily wished she shared the older woman's optimism.
'What did Xavier mean—when he said it was typical of
Ramon to run off?'

Elena shook her head. 'Pay no attention to what Xavier

says. He is hard on people—himself included.' She wrapped her hands around Emily's. 'Ramon is a good man. He will be a good father. Already I see changes in him I never would have imagined.'

Her heart missed a beat. 'Really?'

Elena smiled. 'Really.' She squeezed Emily's hands. 'Sometimes all a man needs is the love of a good woman.'

*Love.*

Emily's heart began to race.

Did she love Ramon?

These last few days, she had started to think she might, and the idea overwhelmed her with a wild, conflicting mix of wonder and fear.

'I've only known you for twenty-four hours, Emily,' Elena continued, 'but I am a good judge of character. I believe you have a kind, forgiving soul. And I believe my son can learn from you.' She cupped Emily's cheek with her palm. 'He fears responsibility, but not for the reasons you might think.'

'Emily.'

Ramon's voice stopped her breath in her lungs. In unison, she and Elena rose and turned.

Rumpled, dishevelled and still breathtakingly handsome in the khaki trousers and black tee shirt he'd worn throughout the day, he strode across the terrace.

He held his hand out to her and, after a brief hesitation, she slipped her hand into his.

His grip was firm as he turned to his mother, his demeanour stiff. 'I apologise for my absence, Mamá.'

Elena reached up and kissed her son's cheek. 'Apology accepted. Now, go. Talk with Emily. You owe her an explanation.'

# CHAPTER ELEVEN

KEEPING HER HAND firmly in his grip, Ramon led Emily into the gardens, along a lighted pathway and into a secluded alcove. Hedges and fragrant rose bushes provided privacy and, to one side, an ornate stone bench sat beneath a high, vine-covered arch.

His blood still beat furiously in his veins from his run-in with Xav.

His brother could be so sanctimonious. So self-righteous, at times.

He let go of Emily and she lifted her hand to his face. 'Ramon…your jaw.'

He seized her wrist and pulled her hand down before she could touch him. 'It's just bruised.'

Frowning, she jerked her wrist free, then hugged her arms around her middle. 'Where have you been?'

He heard the hurt in her voice and his self-hatred burned brighter. Deeper.

But he'd needed the time alone. Time to bring his emotions under control. Time to work out how to explain— how much to tell her.

*All of it*, his conscience cried.

'I hadn't planned to miss dinner,' he said. 'There was a road accident—' Her eyes widened and he quickly added, 'Not me. Tourists.' A group of three young Australian holidaymakers who'd run their camper van off the coastal road and flagged him down in distress. 'I stopped to help and waited until the emergency services arrived.'

Even upset and pale, Emily was beautiful. The mint-green knee-length dress she'd donned for dinner was fresh and feminine, showcasing a figure that was starting to show subtle signs of pregnancy. Her hair was captured loosely at her nape and he knew an overwhelming desire to sink his hands into those lustrous curls, bury his face in them and breathe deeply until her scent overtook his senses and his mind was filled with nothing but her.

He jammed his hands in his pockets and nodded towards the stone bench. 'Sit, Emily.'

Her chin came up, and for a moment he thought she might refuse. Then she sighed and sat down.

He took a deep breath. 'The young man in the tapas bar today was Mateo Mendoza,' he said. 'He's the younger brother of Jorge Mendoza, my best friend during my teens.' He drew another breath but his chest was so tight his lungs wouldn't expand properly. 'When we were eighteen Jorge drowned in a boating accident. Mateo blames me for his brother's death.'

Emily stared at him, wide-eyed. 'Why?'

'Because it was my fault.'

She shook her head. 'I don't understand.'

'It was a reckless teenage escapade. There was alcohol involved. And the boat wasn't seaworthy.' He clenched his jaw against the surge of hated memories. The vision of Jorge's pale, blue-lipped face as he slipped beneath the surface of the ocean, beyond Ramon's desperate reach.

Emily turned her palms up, imploring. 'Ramon. Please. I still don't understand.'

'I was the ringleader,' he bit out. 'And it wasn't the first time I'd led Jorge on some reckless pursuit. His parents had already spoken to mine, expressing their concern.'

She was silent. Then, 'Isn't that what all teenage boys do? Push boundaries? Do reckless things?'

Her attempt to minimise his culpability only fuelled his guilt. She'd heard only half the story. He doubted her sympathy would withstand the rest. He forced himself to go on. He just wanted it out now. Over with.

'I had a girlfriend at the time. Same age, eighteen. After Jorge's funeral, she tried to comfort me but I was in a bad place. I didn't want comfort, so I pushed her away, ended the relationship. I was blunt,' he confessed. 'Cruel, even.' He paused, emotion rising, threatening to engulf him. His throat felt hot and thick. 'She was upset. She went out with her friends and overdosed on a party drug. In the hospital, it was discovered she was five weeks' pregnant.' Shame burned his insides, hot and searing. 'She lost the child.'

'Oh… Ramon…' Emily stared up at him, her features illuminated by silvery moonlight. 'Did she know she was pregnant?'

'No.'

Emily stood up, took a step towards him. 'Which means you didn't, either.'

He frowned. 'That doesn't exonerate me.'

'Of what?' she challenged. 'Ending a relationship? That's not a crime, Ramon.'

He hardened his jaw. 'My actions were callous and ir-responsible.'

'That doesn't make you a murderer.'

'I killed my best friend and my unborn child,' he grated.

She placed her hands on his shoulders. 'You don't really believe that. *I* don't believe that. You were just a teenager.'

'I was old enough to know better. I was reckless. Care-less with the lives of the people I cared about. I hurt Jorge's family. I hurt my girlfriend's family. I hurt *my* family.'

Emily moved closer and he wanted to push her away. Urge her to protect herself. Protect their child.

From *him*.

'You're a good man, Ramon.'

'You don't know that.'

'Yes,' she argued, tilting her chin up. 'I do. When I told you I was pregnant, you could have run. You could have abandoned me. You didn't. You're standing by my side. By our child's side.'

'Don't paint me as a saint, Emily,' he warned. 'I'm not.'

'You're not a monster, either.'

He pinched the bridge of his nose and then remembered it was Xav's favourite gesture and dropped his hand.

'Come to bed,' she said, her voice soft. 'You look exhausted.'

Expelling a heavy breath, he lifted his hand and pushed a stray curl back from her face.

'That's my line,' he growled.

She smiled. Then she caught his hand, interlaced her fingers with his and led him back to the house.

The next day, by mutual agreement, they embarked on their return journey to London sooner than originally planned. Elena was disappointed, but she understood they both wanted to put Saturday's incident behind them and have some time alone to process it.

As their bags were loaded into the SUV that would take them to the airport, she drew Emily aside and embraced her in a tight hug. 'Whatever happens, you and your child— my grandchild—are now part of this family,' she said. 'You will always be welcome here.'

Emily fought hard to stem a rush of tears. In a different life, a make-believe life, she would have grown up with a kind, compassionate mother like Elena. She could only hope she'd be as good a mother to her own child. 'Thank you.'

Elena gripped Emily's arms and gave her a firm look. 'For what it's worth, I believe you and Ramon are going to be fine.'

Not wanting to burst the older woman's bubble, Emily forced a smile. Yesterday, wandering hand in hand with Ramon through the old city, talking and enjoying each other's company as they'd explored the intricate labyrinth of winding streets, she might have agreed. Today, doubt, fear and uncertainty had stripped away any fledgling sense of happiness and hope. Already she could feel an unsettling shift in Ramon, his mood when he'd woken this morning taciturn, remote.

She swallowed, her throat tight. 'How can you be so sure?'

Elena pressed her hand to Emily's cheek. 'Because my son has been running for twelve years,' she said. 'Now he has a reason to stop.'

The journey to the airport was dominated by silence, and as soon as they were in the air Ramon opened his laptop and Emily buried her nose in a magazine.

She didn't absorb a single word.

Instead, her mind replayed every line of every conversation she'd had over the weekend with Ramon and with his mother.

*You have a kind, forgiving soul.*

Did she? She'd never thought of herself as a particularly benevolent person before.

Her mind skipped to her father who'd been AWOL for weeks now and hadn't returned any of her calls.

Was he all right?

She snuck a glance at Ramon, still focused on his screen, and knew he'd be angry if he knew she was worrying over her father's welfare. Her tenuous relationship with Maxwell frustrated Ramon. He didn't understand why she didn't simply sever all connections with her father. She couldn't blame him. Most days she didn't understand it herself.

Where *was* Maxwell? Holed up with a woman somewhere? Deep in some gambling den, perhaps, losing whatever possessions and money he had left to his name?

A familiar feeling of despair washed over her. When it

came to winning her father's attention, she'd never stood a chance against the lure of the high life. For Maxwell, women and high-stakes poker games had proved far more appealing than the responsibilities of fatherhood.

Why had he never settled? Was he running from something? The way Ramon had been running for the last twelve years?

As soon as they'd landed and transferred from the plane to a chauffeured black sedan, Emily fished her phone from her bag. She hadn't checked for messages in more than twenty-four hours. She powered the phone on and held her breath, waiting. Praying.

Seconds later, the air left her lungs on a little exhalation of surprise.

On the screen was a text from Maxwell.

Ramon sent her a questioning look. 'Is something wrong?'

She shook her head. 'No,' she said, and slid her phone back into her bag.

Emily chose a small, quaint restaurant nestled in one of Mayfair's quiet side streets, just a few blocks from The Royce, in which to meet her father. Their phone call, three days previously, had been brief, just long enough for Maxwell to ask if she'd be willing to meet with him and for Emily to agree. He'd turned the choice of time and place over to her and told her to text him the details.

She paused outside the restaurant.

*Would he turn up?*

She stepped inside and Maxwell rose from a table in the rear corner, gesturing to catch her attention.

A dart of surprise shot beneath Emily's ribs. She was ten minutes early, yet he was here waiting for her.

Dry-mouthed, her hands clammy, she propelled her legs forward and made her way over.

Maxwell stayed on his feet, hands by his sides, waiting until Emily had seated herself before taking his chair again.

'You look well, Emily.'

'So do you.'

She couldn't hide her surprise. There were no hollows carved into his cheeks, no dark shadows beneath his eyes. His complexion was healthy, and the whites of his eyes weren't bloodshot. He looked as if he'd spent a month at an exclusive health spa.

'I've been in Switzerland,' he said, as if her expression had broadcasted her thoughts.

'For two months?' The query came out more sharply than she'd intended. But she'd not had a scrap of communication from him until his recent message. It wasn't unusual for him to disappear for weeks on end, but two months was the longest he'd ever gone incommunicado.

'Yes,' he said quietly. 'I was at a private rehab clinic. For gambling and…other addictions.'

Shock suspended Emily's breath. Her gaze went automatically to the table top. There was no whisky tumbler, she realised. No bottle of expensive wine. Just a carafe of water and two glasses.

A waiter approached and Maxwell raised a hand. 'Could we have ten minutes, please?'

When they were alone again, she said, 'I don't know what to say, Maxwell.'

He shook his head. 'There isn't anything you need to say. But, if you're prepared to listen, there are some things I'd like to say to you.'

Emily nodded; she didn't trust herself to speak. Her mouth was too dry, her throat too tight all of a sudden.

'I'm sorry, Emily. I know those words are inadequate,' he said, his voice thick, a little uneven. 'But I want you to know that I am sorry. For everything. You deserved better than me for a father.'

His gaze held hers and she felt as if it was the first time her father had ever looked at her.

*Really* looked at her.

The ache in her throat intensified. She *had* deserved better.

Silence cloaked them for a long moment.

Finally, her voice barely above a whisper, she said, 'Why? Why was it so hard to love me?'

A wretched look crossed his face. 'I wanted to. More than you'll ever know. And I thought maybe I could…after those first few years had passed. But then you started to look so much like her.' His gaze moved slowly over her face, her hair. His look of anguish deepened. 'I couldn't let myself do it. I couldn't risk that kind of pain all over again. If anything had ever happened to you…it would have been like losing Kathryn a second time.'

Her lungs locked again. 'You loved her?'

'More than anything else in this world.' His voice was raw. 'Losing her was the worst thing that's ever happened to me.'

Emily stared at him. The revelation tore through every belief she'd had about her father. 'I… I had no idea.'

A deep frown etched his brow. 'That I loved your mother?'

'How could I have known? You always refused to talk about her.'

'Because it was too painful.'

She rubbed her forehead. 'But…all the women…'

His face reddened. 'When your mother was alive, I was faithful to her, Emily. She was my soul mate. She was irreplaceable… So, after she was gone, I didn't try. I just…'

He let the sentence hang, and Emily thought she understood. He'd resigned himself to casual, meaningless flings because he didn't believe he could love again—or was too afraid to try.

She sucked in a deep breath. Then asked the question she was most afraid to ask. 'Did you blame me for her death?'

Maxwell's chin dropped, agony and shame driving his gaze away from his daughter's. 'Yes.'

The stark admission felt like an all-over body blow, as if someone had dropped her straight into the path of a speeding truck. A part of her understood the psychology of it. Grief could make people irrational. Warp their view of things. Still, it hurt. 'Do you still feel that way?'

His gaze jerked up. 'My God…no. Emily…' He shook his head. 'The fact you look so much like her is still…difficult. But no. It wasn't your fault.'

Her eyes stung, and she blinked back the tears. 'You made me feel unlovable.'

His expression was bleak. 'I don't know how to make that up to you. But I'd like a chance to try.'

'Will you tell me about her?'

'If that's what you'd like.'

Emily thought she'd like that very much.

She took a long sip of water, soothing the burn in her throat. Then she put the glass down and gave him a shaky smile. 'You're going to be a grandfather.'

Maxwell swallowed. 'So I understand. Congratulations, Emily.' He reached across the table and covered her hand briefly with his.

Emily's heart contracted.

The gesture was a long way from a hug.

But it was a start.


When Emily left the restaurant over an hour later, the black sedan and driver that Ramon had insisted she have at her disposal waited on the other side of the street for her.

The driver emerged and opened her door and she sank gratefully into the soft leather.

'Home, Ms Royce?'

'Yes. Thank you.'

Closing her eyes, she let her head fall back against the seat. Her father's unexpected attempt to connect had left her feeling quietly optimistic, but it also heightened the sense that her life was changing at a more dramatic pace than she could handle.

She looked at her watch and sighed. It was barely eight o'clock and she already craved the comfort of her bed.

A comfort she'd soon relinquish, she reminded herself with another flare of unease.

Tomorrow at ten a.m. she would meet with an interior designer at the house in Chelsea to discuss colour schemes and furnishings. Within the month, she and Ramon would be living in their new home and her beloved Wimbledon flat would be rented out to strangers.

Ramon wanted her to sell it.

Emily had refused, then enquired pointedly if he planned to sell his penthouse in Manhattan.

The stand-off had only sharpened the tension between them these last few days.

After thanking and dismissing her driver, she dragged her feet up the stairs and opened the door to her flat, relieved to be home, but also aware of a flutter of trepidation.

Ramon had been deeply unhappy about her meeting with her father and his mood before they'd left for work this morning had been dark and intractable.

Much like his mood every day since their return from Spain, she thought gloomily.

She flipped on a light and put her bag and keys on the hall table before walking through to the lounge. Darkness blanketed the room and suddenly she remembered Ramon had said he was entertaining a business associate at Citrine this evening. Her mind moving to thoughts of hot chocolate and bed, she turned on a lamp—and felt her heart lunge into her throat.

'My God! Ramon!' She clapped her hand over her breast, staring at him as he turned from the window. 'You scared me half to death. Why are you standing in the dark?'

He moved into the lamplight and Emily saw from his face that his mood had not improved from this morning. He still wore his work attire, although his tie and suit jacket had been discarded, and his shirt collar loosened. 'How was dinner with your father?'

His tone was clipped and Emily stifled a sigh. She was exhausted, her emotions drained; she couldn't talk about her conversation with her father, not right this minute, standing here in the middle of the lounge. 'Interesting,' she said, turning towards the kitchen. 'I'm making hot choco-late. Would you like some?'

'I had an interesting meeting, too.'

Reluctantly, she stopped.

'I ran into Carter,' he said.

She frowned. 'Carter…?'

'Ray.' His voice carried an edge of impatience, as though he thought she were being deliberately obtuse. 'Your law-yer.'

'Oh.'

'He offered his congratulations on our engagement and the baby.'

'That's…nice,' she said, the skin at her nape beginning to prickle.

'Asked if we knew yet if it's a boy or a girl.'

The prickling spread into her throat, then her chest, mak-ing it difficult to breathe. 'Ramon…'

'Said if we're expecting a boy,' he barrelled on, as if she hadn't spoken, 'you should notify him so he can prepare to activate your inheritance as soon as the child is born.'

Her breath stopped altogether. *Oh, God.*

He stepped forward, his jaw clenching. When he spoke again, his voice was soft. Dangerous. 'What did he mean, Emily?'

She forced herself to breathe. Told herself it wasn't a big deal. Not to her. Surely it wouldn't be to Ramon?

'There was a…a clause in my grandfather's will. A ridiculous clause,' she added. 'It bequeathed a sum of money to me if certain…stipulations were met.'

His eyes narrowed. 'What kind of stipulations?'

She swallowed, embarrassed. 'If I marry and produce a male heir by the age of thirty.'

She heard his sharp inhale.

'How much?'

'S…sorry?'

'How much money, Emily?' he snapped, and she jumped, unaccustomed to him raising his voice.

'Two million pounds,' she croaked.

'*Dios.*' For a second, incredulity wiped the anger from his face. 'And if you don't?'

'I forfeit the inheritance. The money goes to charity.' She shifted her feet under his hardening stare. 'I'm sorry I didn't tell you about it sooner, but it's not important to me, Ramon. It was my grandfather's eccentric attempt to ensure his legacy eventually passes to a male heir. I couldn't care less about that money.'

The hard gleam in his eyes remained. 'Does your father know about the clause?'

She hesitated. 'Yes.'

'And what did he want tonight?' The cynical twist of his lips made his implication shockingly clear.

She took a step back from him, her insides wrenching. '*No.*' The word burst from her, almost a shout. She gave her head a vigorous shake. 'You're wrong.'

He grasped her wrist, halting her retreat. 'Don't be naive, Emily,' he said tersely.

'I'm not being naive. You're being twisted and cynical. And unfair!' She tried to pull free but he held fast. 'You have no idea what happened between my father and me tonight.'

'Then tell me.' He tugged her close and cupped his other hand under her jaw, forcing her gaze up to his. 'Convince me he hasn't crawled out of the woodwork after two months hoping to benefit from your potential windfall.'

'That accusation is disgusting.' Her voice trembled with outrage. His scepticism cast an icy pall over her optimism. Worse, it filled her head with horrible, stomach-shredding doubts. 'My father has been in a rehab clinic for the last two months, if you must know. He's getting himself together. And yes—' she stared at him defiantly '—he wants to reconcile.'

He gave a low, grating laugh. 'Like I said, *querida*. Naive.'

His mocking tone drove a dagger of hurt into her thundering heart.

Ramon never spoke to her like this.

Not the Ramon she knew.

*Not the Ramon she loved.*

But he'd not been the same man since Spain, had he? The awful incident with his friend's brother had affected him on some deep level, somewhere far beyond the limit of her reach.

'I don't think this...this *mood* of yours is about my father at all,' she challenged. 'I think it's about you.'

As though she were suddenly radioactive, he released her and stepped back. 'What the hell does that mean?'

'It means you don't believe you're worthy of forgiveness, so you don't think anyone else is either.'

A savage frown furrowed his brow. 'Forgiveness must be earned, Emily.'

'Is that what you've been doing, Ramon? Earning forgiveness these last twelve years?' His expression darkened but she forged on. 'Is that why you gave up your architectural career to join the family business? Why you set your sights on The Royce? Is it all about earning brownie points so your family forgives you?'

'Emily.' His voice was a low growl.

She ignored the warning. 'Do you know what the crazy thing is? You have amazing parents who love you, but you're so busy keeping them at arm's length you haven't noticed they forgave you a long time ago.'

'Enough!' He slashed his hand through the air. 'This *is* about your father. And I forbid you to see him.'

Disbelieving laughter tore from her throat. 'You can't stop me seeing my father, Ramon.' Before he said anything else that further shredded her heart, she spun on her heel and stormed into the kitchen.

Ten seconds later, she heard the front door slam. The sound echoed through the empty flat and through her chest like the final, crippling thrust of his knife into her heart.

Ramon found a pub in the local village, wedged himself into a dimly lit corner and nursed a glass of single malt until his temper had cooled.

*Dios.* Why was she so stubborn? So blind? So willing to give her father yet another chance?

Maxwell was a gambler. Was it not obvious to her that he was playing an angle? Playing *her*?

Protectiveness surged, fierce and overwhelming. He believed her about the money not mattering to her. If it had, she would have wanted to know their child's sex as soon as possible, yet she had told the specialist she'd prefer to wait until the birth.

But not to question the timing of Maxwell's desire to reconcile was insanity.

Perhaps they *should* find out the baby's gender. It would

put the matter to rest. If it was a girl, and Maxwell's enthusiasm for connecting with his daughter suddenly waned, it would dispel any illusions.

And break Emily's heart at the same time.

He pushed his empty glass away and rose, regret scything through him.

He'd seen the look on her face when he had questioned Maxwell's motives. He knew the sour mood he hadn't shaken off since their disastrous weekend in Barcelona had lent his tongue a harsh, uncharacteristic edge. He'd hurt her. Which went against the grain of everything he was trying to achieve.

And then she'd lashed back.

*I think it's about you.*

His feet pounded the pavement, frustration congealing in his gut as he stalked the streets back to the flat. She'd seen him with his family for all of thirty-six hours and thought she understood him.

She understood nothing.

*Nothing.*

When he arrived, she was waiting up, sitting in the window seat she favoured for quiet reflection. Her glorious golden hair flowed loose and a pair of flannel pyjamas swamped her delectable curves. He suspected the attire was a deliberate attempt to discourage him from intimacy. It didn't work. He wanted to bundle her into his arms. Carry her to bed and make passionate love to her until the hurt and anger on her face dissolved into something else.

His desire only deepened his frustration. Intensified the sense he was waging a losing battle within himself. Every part of him felt at odds. His emotions. His instincts. His desires.

He wanted to protect her. From her father. From the world. From anything and anyone who dared to threaten the wellbeing of her and their child. But he also wanted to distance himself from her. Protect her from himself. From his inherent ability to hurt the people he loved.

And Ramon had come to suspect that what he felt for this woman was raw, terrifying, unadulterated love.

'I can't marry you, Ramon.'

He blinked, her statement skating over his thoughts, taking a moment to register. 'What?'

She uncurled from the cushions, stood and faced him. 'You told me I wouldn't have to do this alone.'

He shook his head, confused. 'You don't. I'm here, Emily.'

'Are you?' She stared at him, her eyes gigantic pools of anguished grey in her pale face. 'Because these last few days, it's felt as if you've been somewhere else. As if you've erected a wall I can't see over, or through.'

'That's not true.' His denial was abrupt. Hoarse.

'It is,' she disputed. 'And this business with my father—with the inheritance—it's all just a smokescreen for the deeper issue.'

Exasperation had him throwing up his hands. 'Not this again.'

'Yes, Ramon. *This* again. You have to forgive yourself and move on.' She took a deep breath. 'I learned something about my father tonight. He's been running for a long time. Choosing the lifestyle he has because he's afraid to love and lose again, the way he lost my mother. I think you're running too, Ramon.'

Her comparison with him to Maxwell cut to the bone. His nostrils flared. 'I'm here, Emily,' he repeated. 'I haven't run since the day you told me you were pregnant.'

'Not physically.' She stepped forward, pressing her hand against the centre of his chest. 'But in here…you're afraid. Afraid to get too close to people in case you hurt them.'

'You're talking nonsense,' he gritted out.

The look of utter sadness crossing her face sliced a

sharp, unbearable pain through his chest. She dropped her hand. 'I'm in love with you, Ramon,' she said, and the words robbed his lungs of breath. 'You're the father of my baby and you're a good man. I want to marry you, share a home, raise our child together. But I can't be with you if you're going to be emotionally distant, the way you are with your family. I—we—' she placed her hand over the gentle swell of her belly '—deserve better.'

She twisted the diamond and sapphire engagement ring off her left hand.

'Emily…'

'I've put your things in the spare room. You can stay to-night—or not. Up to you. But I want you to leave tomorrow. Take some time and decide if you're ready to stop running. Until then—' she put the ring on the coffee table '—I think you should hold onto this.'

# CHAPTER TWELVE

So FAR EMILY had waited five days, and they'd been the longest, most misery-filled days of her life.

She missed Ramon. Every hour. Every minute. Every second of every day.

The weekend had been the worst. The home she usually adored had felt cold and soulless, and even an afternoon of baking had failed to stir any joy.

And now, back in the office, seated at her desk and staring listlessly at her screen, work wasn't proving the distraction she'd hoped for either.

Her stomach churned with doubt and fear.

She'd taken an enormous risk by confessing her love to her baby's father then sending him away.

Had she made a terrible mistake?

She hadn't wanted him to stay away. She'd wanted him to go and take a long, hard look inside himself and then come back to her.

*And tell her he loved her.*

Because she wouldn't settle for less. For too many years she had pined for love. She couldn't waste the rest of her life pining for his. He'd always have a place in their child's life—she'd never deny her child its father—but she could not marry a man who didn't love her.

Emily's phone pinged. Shutting off her thoughts, she delved into her bag and pulled out her phone.

And froze.

Her heart climbed into her throat.

*Ramon.*

His message was short.

A car is waiting outside for you. See Marsha on your way out.

She frowned at the screen. He'd made her wait five days and these were the words with which he'd chosen to communicate with her first? Hands shaking, she texted back.

It's 3.30 p.m. on a Monday. I'm working.

His response was immediate.

Finish early.

Heart pounding, she chewed her lip, then forced her thumbs to work again.

Where am I going?

It's a surprise.

I don't like surprises.

Humour me.

She stared at the screen for a long moment, her tummy taut with indecision. When the phone pinged again, she jumped.

Please.

She hesitated, but her resistance was already melting, her desire to see him too powerful, too overwhelming. Releasing a pent-up breath, she fired back an 'OK'.

Outside the office, Marsha rose from her desk, her cheeks flushing pink. 'I'm sorry,' she said, holding out Emily's passport. 'He said I wasn't to warn you.'

A flicker of excitement and hope skimmed through Emily's stomach before she quickly dampened the hazardous feelings. She had no idea what he'd say to her when she saw him. She'd be a fool to allow hope to soar only then to find her heart painfully crushed.

Still, the fluttering in her stomach grew more intense during the ride to the airport. Not even the short, sharp jab of disappointment she felt when she boarded Ramon's plane and saw he wasn't there could diminish the jittery feeling of anticipation for very long.

The male flight attendant brought her an orange juice. 'It's nice to see you again, Ms Royce.'

She managed a smile. 'And you. Umm… Could you tell me where we're going, please?'

His polite expression didn't alter. 'Paris,' he said. 'We should be there in fifty-five minutes.'

By the time Emily climbed out of the back of a shiny limo in front of Saphir, her mouth was bone-dry and her palms so damp she had to repeatedly wipe them down the front of her simple black dress. A smiling concierge greeted her, escorted her inside and led her to the same lift she'd ridden with Ramon three months earlier.

She stepped in and gripped the handrail.

*Only three months?*

It felt like a lifetime ago.

The lift bore her swiftly upwards and when she stepped out into the penthouse, feeling breathless and a little light-headed, he was there.

Her feet stumbled to a stop.

Clean-shaven and wearing dark trousers and a pale blue open-necked shirt, he looked as vital and bone-meltingly beautiful as he had on that fateful late summer night when he'd brought her here.

Their gazes locked and she began to tremble, desire and

nervous excitement pin-wheeling through her in a potent, knee-weakening mix.

Then, abruptly, he pulled his hands from his pockets and strode towards her, his steps long and purposeful. He halted in front of her and cradled her face in his hands, and just that simple touch catapulted her senses into overdrive.

'Did you miss me, Emily?'

*Oh, so much.* She feigned a shrug of indifference. 'Not really.'

His eyes gleamed. 'Not at all?'

'Maybe a little bit,' she whispered.

They both faintly smiled. It was the same exchange they'd had in her kitchen more than three weeks ago when he'd returned from Paris—moments before they'd had scorching hot sex in her room.

'I missed you.' He drew his thumbs across her cheeks, lowered his forehead to hers.

Emily felt her insides melting. Felt little tendrils of hope weaving around her heart. She dropped her bag, lifted her hands and curled them over his strong, masculine wrists. 'Where have you been?'

He raised his head. 'I went back to Spain.'

'What for?'

His hands lowered, settling around her waist, drawing her close. 'I had some ghosts to lay to rest. Some people to visit.'

'Including your parents?'

'Including my parents.'

Emily's thoughts flickered to Elena and her heart swelled with gladness for the other woman. 'And did you make any discoveries?'

'A few.'

His heart pumping at a fierce pace, Ramon studied the exquisite features of the woman who had boldly declared her love for him, then sent him packing and told him not to return until he'd figured himself out.

She'd shocked him to his core. Flipped him into a brutal tailspin of anger and disbelief.

And fear. Mind-bending, gut-wrenching fear—because he'd known he couldn't lose her.

'I learned,' he said, 'that sometimes a man must confront his past before he can put it behind him.'

Soft grey eyes searched his. 'And have you?'

'*Sí, querida*. I have.'

Tears filled her eyes then and, though he had no wish to see her cry, he took them as a good sign.

'Who else did you visit?'

'Many people,' he confessed.

He had started with his old girlfriend, with whom, once he'd tracked her down, he'd had the conversation they should've had twelve years ago before he'd fled Spain. He'd found Ana in a stylish home in Madrid, married with two small children, and happy. She'd moved on and she bore Ramon no ill will. Next he'd visited Jorge's parents in Barcelona, whom he'd not seen since the funeral, and discovered they didn't share their youngest son's antipathy towards Ramon. Jorge's mother had hugged him, cried for a moment, then invited him in. Matteo, they'd said, was a troubled young man, and they'd been appalled to hear of the incident in the tapas bar.

The next day he'd gone to see his brother, and then he'd returned to his parents' villa, where, for the first time in a long time, he'd looked his mother in the eye and embraced her in a hug that had lifted her feet clean off the ground.

Finally, he'd come back to London and had a long, frank conversation with Maxwell Royce.

It'd been an intense, cathartic five days, and at some point he'd tell it all to Emily, but not now. That was the past. Right now his interest lay only in the future.

'Want to know what else I learned, *querida*?' he asked softly.

She nodded, and he reached into his pocket, pulling out the black velvet box containing her engagement ring.

'I learned that I'm tired of running...' He plucked the ring from its bed, lifted her left hand and slid the cool platinum band with its striking setting of diamonds and sapphires onto her finger. 'And that I want to be the man—the *only* man—who loves you for the rest of his life.' He pressed his lips to her knuckles. 'I love you, *mi belleza*. Will you do me the honour of becoming my wife?'

Eyes glistening, she wound her arms around his neck, her delicious curves pressing into his body. 'Yes,' she said, and a groan of relief mingled with desire tore from Ramon's throat.

Gathering her close, he claimed her mouth in a kiss that was almost savage in its intensity.

Long minutes later, when their breath-deprived lungs cried out for air, they broke apart.

Surrendering to the feverish need to stamp his possession on her in every way possible, he swung her into his arms and headed for the bedroom.

As he lowered her onto the bed, she captured his jaw in her hand and murmured, 'Why Paris?'

He laid his hand over her stomach, the small bump which he couldn't wait to see grow filling his palm. 'This is where we began. Where we created our child.' He trailed his lips along her jaw, down her neck. 'It will be a special place for us always, *si*?'

Her eyes filled again. 'I love you, Ramon.'

Fierce emotion flooded him. 'Say it again,' he demanded roughly against her throat.

Her laughter was pure. Sweet. 'I love you.' Insistent hands tugged his shirt tails from his trousers. 'Your turn,' she whispered.

He slid his hand under her dress, his questing fingers moving over heated, quivering skin. 'I love you, *mi belleza*.'

She arched under his touch.

'Show me,' she urged.

And he did.

# EPILOGUE

WITH A GLASS of chilled Prosecco in her hand, Marsha slipped away from the lively gathering taking place in the big, sunny back garden of Emily and Ramon's Chelsea home and crossed the bright green lawn towards the house.

She stepped into the kitchen and her gaze fell on the home-made custard tart over which Emily was grating fresh nutmeg. 'Yum! That looks delicious.' She shifted her attention to the large kitchen table where Emily and Ramon often shared their meals instead of in the formal dining room. This afternoon, savouries and cakes and slices and tarts crowded the table's surface. 'I can't believe you did all of this yourself.'

'I had some help from my housekeeper,' Emily confided.

Marsha's eyebrows rose. 'You have a housekeeper?'

'A part-time one,' she said. 'Ramon insisted. It was either that or a nanny and I refused the latter.'

Marsha put her glass down on the bench and cast her gaze around the gorgeous designer kitchen. 'I miss you at work but I can't blame you for not rushing back.' She gave a wistful smile. 'Do you think you'll ever return?'

Emily's shrug was non-committal. 'I haven't decided yet,' she admitted, her feelings on the matter mixed. The club and her role there had been her life for so many years, and she'd expected to miss it, but she had other priorities now. Priorities that filled a void she hadn't realised existed and which meant a great deal more to her than The Royce.

A small, plaintive wail pierced the air and Emily's maternal instincts went on instant alert.

Elena de la Vega entered the kitchen, making shushing, soothing sounds to the tiny bundle in her arms. 'I think my granddaughter has already tired of her christening party,' she said to Emily, her lovely face awash with pride and pleasure as she handed over her grandchild.

Emily smiled her thanks. 'I'll feed her and settle her for a nap and then i'll be out.' She glanced at Marsha. 'Would you do me a favour and let everyone know they can help themselves to food?'

She climbed the elegant curved staircase and made her way to the light-filled nursery, an intense joy ballooning in her chest as she gazed down at her daughter.

Kathryn Georgina de la Vega—Katie, to her parents— had arrived ten weeks ago, exactly three months from the day her parents had wed in a beautiful church in Barcelona. The wedding and reception, attended by hundreds of guests, had been a larger, more elaborate affair than Emily had wanted, but the de la Vegas were a prominent family in Spain, and she'd quickly understood her hopes for a small, private ceremony were unrealistic. Plus, Elena's enthusiasm for the planning had been both irrepressible and contagious. Emily hadn't had the heart to restrain her.

She'd invited Marsha and her management team to the wedding and, to her surprise, they'd all come, but the person whose presence had mattered to Emily the most had been her father's. He'd given her away and as he'd walked her down the aisle in her stunning gown of ivory silk and French lace, cleverly styled to hide her baby bump, she'd been fairly sure she'd seen a tear shining in his eye.

Of course her relationship with her father remained a work in progress. Twenty-eight years of hurt wouldn't heal overnight. But they were moving in the right direction and even Ramon was thawing towards him, especially now the inheritance issue had been temporarily sidelined.

Emily finished nursing then drifted to the window with Katie nestled in her arms, humming the tune of the Spanish lullaby Ramon crooned to his daughter every night.

Chatter and laughter floated up from the garden, along with the squeals and shouts of their neighbours' children—Joshua and Maddie—who chased each other through the trees at the rear of the property. Amidst the clusters of people Marsha chatted with Maddie and Joshua's mother, Tamsin, who'd become a friend to Emily, while Elena, a natural-born conversationalist, talked with Marsha's boyfriend and Tamsin's husband. Seated in the shade of a large oak tree, Vittorio and her father conversed and, further away beneath a different tree, Ramon and his brother appeared deep in conversation.

Whatever they spoke about it must have been serious, for the expressions on their faces were intense.

Emily still marvelled that Xavier, an incurable workaholic, had taken time out of his demanding schedule to visit London.

Suddenly Ramon looked up and caught her eye through the glass and her breath hitched. Her husband seemed to possess a sixth sense where she was concerned; rarely did she get to observe him without his noticing.

She watched him grip his brother's shoulder, say something and then stride across the lawn towards the house. By the time he walked into the nursery, she'd settled their daughter down to sleep and returned to the window. He leaned over the cot, kissed a rosy little cheek and then moved behind his wife, sliding his arms around her middle.

She leaned her head against his shoulder, her gaze focused on the figure of his handsome, enigmatic brother, standing alone beneath the tree now. 'Is everything all right with Xav?'

Ramon kissed the top of her head. 'He's fine.'

'He doesn't look fine,' she said. 'He looks...lonely.'

Ramon gave a soft snort. 'My brother isn't lonely.'

'How do you know?'

He turned her in his arms and looked down at her. 'How

about more focus on your husband and less on his brother?' he growled.

Emily hid a smile. Her husband's occasional displays of jealousy always amused her. 'Fine,' she whispered, conscious of their daughter sleeping. 'Let's join our guests, then.'

She went to move but his arms tightened, locking her in his hold. He dropped a kiss on her mouth that stole her breath with its tenderness, then raised his head. 'Happy?' he queried softly.

This time she let her smile show. How could she be anything else? She had a family, people she loved, people who loved *her*. And she had this beautiful home that was already filling with love, laughter and joy.

Their 'for ever' home.

She wrapped her arms around his neck and kissed him. 'Blissfully.'

\* \* \* \* \*

*If you enjoyed*
*A NIGHT, A CONSEQUENCE, A VOW*
*why not explore these other Angela Bissell stories?*

*SURRENDERING TO THE VENGEFUL ITALIAN*
*DEFYING HER BILLIONAIRE PROTECTOR*
*Available now!*

*And look out for Xavier's story, part two of the*
*RUTHLESS BILLIONAIRE BROTHERS DUET*
*Coming soon!*

# MILLS & BOON®

# MODERN™

**POWER, PASSION AND IRRESISTIBLE TEMPTATION**

# MILLS & BOON®

## *EXCLUSIVE EXTRACT*

Reluctant Sheikh Salim Al-Noury would rather abdicate
than taint the realm with his dark secrets.

But could one exquisitely beautiful diplomat convince
him otherwise?...

Christmas means heartbreak to Charlotte, and this over-
seas assignment offers the perfect getaway. But Salim
proves to be her most challenging client yet, and his
rugged masculinity awakens untouched Charlotte to
unimaginable pleasures!

*Read on for a sneak preview of Abby Green's book*
**A CHRISTMAS BRIDE FOR THE KING**
Rulers of the Desert

She looked Salim straight in the eye. 'Life is so easy for
you, isn't it? No wonder you don't want to rule—it would
put a serious cramp in your lifestyle and a dent in your
empire. Have you *ever* had to think of anyone but yourself,
Salim? Have you *ever* had to consider the consequences of
your actions? People like you make me—'

'Enough.' Salim punctuated the harshly spoken word by
taking her arms in his hands. He said it again. 'Enough,
Charlotte. You've made your point.'

She couldn't breathe after the way he'd just said her
name. *Roughly.* His hands were huge on her arms, and firm
but not painful. She knew she should say *Let me go* but
somehow the words wouldn't form in her mouth.

Salim's eyes were blazing down into hers and for a
second she had the impression that she'd somehow...*hurt*
him. But in the next instant any coherent thought fled,

because he slammed his mouth down onto hers and all she was aware of was shocking heat, strength, and a surge of need such as she'd never experienced before.

Salim couldn't recall when he'd felt angrier—people had thrown all sorts of insults at him for years. Women who'd expected more than he'd been prepared to give. Business adversaries he'd bested. His brother. His parents. But for some reason this buttoned-up slender woman with her cool judgmental attitude was getting to him like no one else ever had.

The urge to kiss her had been born out of that anger and a need to stop her words, but also because he'd felt a hot throb of desire that had eluded him for so long he'd almost forgotten what it felt like.

Her mouth was soft and pliant under his, but on some dim level not clouded red with lust and anger he knew it was shock—and, sure enough, after a couple of seconds he felt her tense and her mouth tighten against his.

He knew he should draw back.

If he was another man he might try to convince himself he'd only intended the kiss to be a display of power, but Salim had never drawn back from admitting his full failings. And he couldn't pull back—not if a thousand horses were tied to his body. Because he wanted her.

*Don't miss*
**A CHRISTMAS BRIDE FOR THE KING**
By Abby Green

Available December 2017

www.millsandboon.co.uk